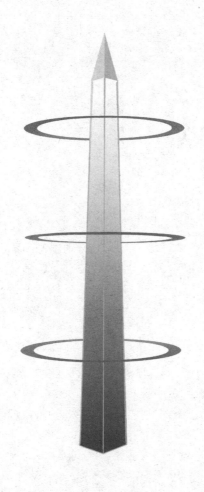

LAST GATE
OF THE EMPEROR
THE ROYAL TRIALS

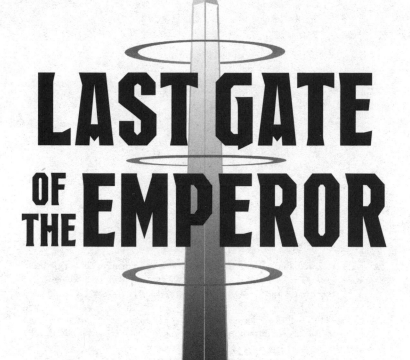

LAST GATE OF THE EMPEROR

THE ROYAL TRIALS

KWAME MBALIA
PRINCE JOEL MAKONNEN

SCHOLASTIC PRESS

NEW YORK

All rights reserved. Published by Scholastic Press, an imprint of Scholastic Inc.,
Publishers since 1920. SCHOLASTIC, SCHOLASTIC PRESS, and associated logos are
trademarks and/or registered trademarks of Scholastic Inc.

The publisher does not have any control over and does not assume any
responsibility for author or third-party websites or their content.

This book is a work of fiction. Names, characters, places, and incidents
are either the product of the author's imagination or are used fictitiously, and
any resemblance to actual persons, living or dead, business establishments, events,
or locales is entirely coincidental.

Library of Congress Cataloging-in-Publication Data available

ISBN 978-1-338-66595-6

1 2022

Printed in the U.S.A.   23
First edition, July 2022

Book design by Elizabeth B. Parisi

TO THE CHILDREN STILL SEARCHING FOR THEIR PLACE IN THE STORY.

LAST GATE
OF THE EMPEROR
THE ROYAL TRIALS

Automated voice: Checking approved holofeeds for today, 2150.227.

Automated voice: No feeds approved. Prisoner restricted at quantum levels.

Automated voice: Unauthorized access detected.

Automated voice: Processing . . . processing . . . proc

Automated voice: Access granted. Welcome, USER_ID_NOT_FOUND.

Automated voice: Three feeds approved. Playing first holofeed.

INA Newsbot: Intergalactic News Association. News from the stars you can trust. Now this.

INA Newsbot: Excitement! Speculation! And more than a little curiosity, as an empire returns. Axum, long thought destroyed, has reemerged. But is the former benevolent superpower what it once was? Even now, as the iconic traveling space station enters the edges of the Sol-Luna System, people are divided.

INA Newsbot: Some welcome the return of the creators of much of the technology we currently use, including this newsbot. Others can't help but point out their convenient timing, just as the Inter-galactic Union is set to vote on who will be awarded all the scientific research left behind when Axum disappeared. And just where were they? Why do preliminary scans show battle damage on the space station? And, as several IU ambassadors have men-tioned privately, what do they want? These questions and more will have to be answered, and soon.

INA Newsbot: And now this: Another inner-system attack by the group calling themselves the Shrikes. IU authority says—

Automated voice: End of first holofeed.

Automated voice: Playing second holofeed.

nanoL0gic: Welcooooooooome to a special episode of *epiCast*! Coming to you live from the Jupiter Colony Academy! Thank you to our partners at LunaCola—because of them, we're now streaming throughout Sol System.

nanoL0gic: The Royal Trials are almost here. Are you ready? We'll have highlights and commentary from games across the tournament. I'm your host,

L0giiiiic, and it's time for my favorite segment and yours, "Stream Hopping"! So plug in, get your questions ready, and hold on to your digitized butts, because YOU might get to hop in stream with me. Ready? Let's gooooo!

nanoL0gic: Hey, what's up, you're holo'ed in the *epiCast* stream. What's your name, and what're you most excited about?

Bank$hot: Hey, I'm on! I'm on! MOM! Holy . . . okay, hey, L0gic! My name is Bank$hot, I'm eleven, and I'm super excited about the Royal Trials, especially the Trios.

nanoL0gic: Hey, Bank$hot, welcome to the stream! And Trios! Definitely ready to see our faves compete. If for some chaffing reason you don't know what Trios is, jack up the volume on the stream and pay attention. Trios is the new battle royale format—not one, not two, but three players team up in squad-based action to take on other teams, all competing to reach the final level. But the fun doesn't end there! Once at the final level, it's every player for themselves! Ultimate betrayals and backstabbing! If you thought the rivalries were heated in Duos, look out! Thanks, Bank$hot!

nanoL0gic: Hey, what's up? You're holo'ed in the *epiCast* stream. What's your name, and what're you most excited about?

Imanl: Heeeey, L0gic. My name is Imanl, and I'm ready to meet the new prince! Do you think he'll make an appearance? Ooh, do you think he'll play in the Royal Trials?

nanoL0gic: Hey, Imanl, nice holofit! And the prince! What a story, right? Royalty at the battle royale. The headlines stream themselves! Prince Yared the First, better known as Yared the Gr8, is one of the top gamers across the leaderboards, especially the HKO. I sure hope he enters the Trials. But who knows? No one's seen or heard from him since Axum entered the system. Will one of the galaxy's top gamers miss out on the tournament of a lifetime? Where is Prince Yared?

nanoL0gic: Where is Prince Yared?

nanoL0gic: Where is Prince Yared?

nanoL0gic: Where aazzse22&^2 . . . .

Automated voice: Holofeed corrupted. End of holofeed.

Automated voice: Playing third holofeed.

. . .

. . .

. . .

The Fallen: They're here . . . It's time.

Automated voice: End of holofeed.

Log Entry, 0923 ST, Private Diary of the Royal Heir, Lij Yared Heywat

I, Yared Heywat—recently discovered prince of the Axum Empire, and not-so-recently-discovered top-ranked gamer on any leaderboard you can name—am formally using this diary entry as my personal confession.

First, I did not mean to start an intergalactic incident with an entire nation of artificial intelligences. I love sentient AIs. One of my best friends, a bionic lioness, is a sentient AI. The Coalition of Sentient Intelligence Networks has my deepest apologies, and I will do my best to support them going forward. I even bought an *I Love CoSIN* pin for my flight suit.

Second, I 100 percent believed that solar collector I destroyed was already broken. To the wonderful LiquiBulb corporation (I'm a huge fan of your juice bulbs, by the way—super refreshing and tasty, ten out of ten, would buy for my friends), I am super-duper sorry. Hopefully power will be restored to your facility soon and we all will get to enjoy . . . your spinach-and-salmon-soufflé juice bulbs once again. Mmm. I can taste the energy already. Lovely.

Finally, to the person whom I will actually be sending this diary entry but can't actually name because some bionic lionesses like to read my outgoing comms for "protection," I'm sorry. I really am. But, if I had to do it all again, every single action taken up to this point, you know what? I would.

Even the part where I nearly died.

CHAPTER ONE

0645 ST, Harar Station, Axum

The shrieking alarm caught me with my pants down. Literally. Look, I don't like telling you any more than you like hearing it, but the truth is the truth. And my Royal Education Adviser and Reminder constantly begs me to tell the honest truth. Not boast, brag, or stretch it in any way. And I don't know about you, but I listen to my REAR.

"Azaj, what's going on?" I asked, fumbling with my formal flight suit. It's hard to put on a uniform while hovering upside down in midair. More on that in a second.

The Harar's minister of the palace—an AI assistant that lived in Axum's servers—appeared as a translucent hologram in front of me and frowned. "It appears that you need help dressing, among other things."

"Not my status—the station!" I snapped. "What's the emergency?"

The hologram sniffed. Can holograms sniff? Azaj, when

it had to appear in front of people, took on the image of a thin older man with a pencil-thin graying mustache and a shimmering green shamma. The long cloth twisted and wrapped around the AI in a formal pattern, an arrangement I couldn't hope to imitate. I should know, because it's what I was currently wrangling with.

Upside down, again. I promise I'll explain why in a second.

"I shall brief you once you've extricated yourself from your current predicament. As an aside, Her Royal Highness—your mother—instructed me to collect you. And to, I quote, 'tell him to stop trying to cheat. He'll still lose during family game night, regardless of whatever hacks he uploads to his nefasi.'"

I folded my arms and glared at the hologram, but Azaj merely lifted an eyebrow. I guess it's hard to appear intimidating when you're wearing nothing but high-tech undies and floating upside down.

"I wasn't trying to cheat," I grumbled.

Explanation time, because I don't want anyone saying Yared the Gr8 is a cheater. I have to protect my rep—people already thought I got an unfair advantage, what with being a prince and all.

I was currently hovering high above the Meshenitai simulation room. It was a large oval space the size of a field. The walls sloped out and up in a gentle curve, with silver lines forming a checkered pattern against the soft gray. When activated, the room could simulate any environment, under any conditions you could think of. Want to pilot a powered exoskeleton (exo for short) around a tropical island? What about through an abandoned battle cruiser that crashed on a moon? The possibilities were endless, and I spent hours coming up with different scenarios. Days sometimes. Just . . . me. By myself. Coming up with ridiculous tasks and trying to complete them.

The Ibis used to help me program them, but ever since she started her Meshenitai astrogator training, she had less and less time to hang out. Uncle Moti used it to train Meshenitai in different maneuvers, but he'd been called away for some important meeting a few days ago. I hadn't seen him since. In fact, I hadn't really seen anyone over the past few days. Even Besa, my bionic lioness turned Guardian, a half-ton bodyguard with diranium claws and a ticklish spot behind her ears, was gone a lot. Something about getting new claw upgrades. I don't know, that cat was always getting her nails done.

The point is I was . . . I was lonely. There. I said it. Nobody tells you that being a prince means missing gaming sessions with friends because you have to learn protocol. So to help out, Mom, the Empress, came up with family game night. I got to pick the game, and we all—me, Uncle Moti, Dad, Mom, the Ibis, and Besa—would trek to the simulator and laugh, eat snacks, and game.

Nobody also told me that Mom was a genius when it came to capture the flag. Seriously. It was borderline unbelievable. Have you ever played CTF in an exo? You have to stay on your toes, and Mom was a pro.

So that's why I was in there, late for dinner, upside down in my nefasi as the mysterious alarm blared and the simulation froze. Practice. Not that Azaj cared. The virtual minister's responsibilities—making sure every part of Axum Station ran smoothly—didn't include listening to my excuses.

By the way the hologram was tapping a virtual finger impatiently, a certain newly discovered prince was complicating things.

You can take the boy out of Addis Prime, but you can't take Addis Prime out of the boy.

"Just give me two seconds, Azaj, and I'll be ready. They gave me a defective shamma. Am I supposed to wrap it over the arm or under the arm?"

"You're supposed to be on the ground right side up when you put it on," the AI said drily.

"That's boring." I finally managed to pull the cloth into position and grinned. "See? Just your esteemed presence helps me out. By the way, have you seen my REAR?"

Azaj winced. "I wish you wouldn't call it that."

"'Every good prince's REAR should always be right behind him,'" I quoted from the orientation holovid I had to watch when the adviser bot was assigned to me. "'Backing him up.'"

Azaj scowled, then the hologram straightened at its edges. It began to shimmer. "It appears I am being summoned. Possibly because of the station-wide alert that was just issued. I would suggest, my prince, that you familiarize yourself with station protocols before leaving your quarters. And not just the ones that are in place during an emergency. Day-to-day ones, such as dressing in appropriate attire, are also important. I will send your REAR—oh, teff of the saints, now he's got me calling it that. Your *adviser* should be along shortly."

With that, the AI palace minister disappeared, and so did the grin on my face. There was so much I didn't know about being a prince. Sooner or later, it was going to catch up with me. I just hoped it wouldn't be in front of anyone.

Okay, you guys, I'm back with another update. I hope you all liked the last one. It felt kinda nice talking to y'all, even though you can't talk back. Anyway, enough of that dull stuff. Listen up, here are Yared's Top Ten Facts You Didn't Know about Being a Space Prince:

1. Talking!

Everybody wants to talk to me. Wait, I don't think that's right. Everybody wants to talk AT me. It's like all the newsvid reporters want to talk to the new prince about Axum and what my daily routine is and stuff like that. I think one group even sent a camera-drone by one-way courier rocket to have it follow me around for a day in the life of Prince Yared.

But no one actually wants to have a conversation with me, you know? It's like, they don't want to talk to Yared—just "the prince." Does that makes sense? Anyway.

2. Space!

Not the stars and planets and that asteroid I got to name. (Hope you like the Haji-0043 vids I linked.) I'm talking about all the room there is aboard the Harar. That's the name of the top section of the Axum capital space station. There are two more modules still missing, and we're heading to find one of them, Adwa, now. Maybe there will be a bunch of kids living there when we arrive. It'd be nice to have some people in all this space. I mean, yeah, it's cool to have my own room and not hear Uncle Moti snoring and Besa having that one dream where she fights a bunamech for the last bulb of lubricant oil. But it'd be nice to have some more people to hang out with in all this space, too.

Wow, this is getting kind of sad. That's not the point of these updates! Okay, the next one should be really cool.

3. Medical tattoos!

Okay, technically they're miniature med-drones that are assigned to check my vitals, give me vitamins, and make sure I have the latest antibiotics. But still. They draw them onto your skin, and you can pick the pattern you want! It's only right, since no one really likes robugs crawling around them. (That name is patent-pending, by the way, so don't steal it.)

The robugs are super important, apparently, because did you know there are, like, millions of things that can get you sick if you travel the galaxy? It's like every world has their own version of the flu and they're just itching to give it to you.

Anyway, that's it for now. I gotta go; there's somebody coming. I'll drop this off at the next Nexus uplink I see. Later, guys!

My REAR found me frozen in a desert.

No, seriously, I'm not joking. All the birr a royal allowance provided, and I couldn't get a decent holosim to work. There I was, Prince Yared of Axum—an empire of advanced technology and sparkling ingenuity—floating helplessly two hundred meters up in the air.

Upside down, mind you!

The harness of my nefasi, the backpack I lined with anti-gravity padding, held me high above the space station's sim chamber floor. Technically I wasn't supposed to be here. The Meshenitai, fabled warriors and protectors of Axum, trained here. Battle scenarios, space station defense, rescue strategies—they all could be programmed to play out in thousands of different environments. If my uncle Moti—excuse me, General Moti Berihun, commander of the Burning Legion of Axum—caught me here, I'd be doing laps around the docking ring for hours.

Good thing he was off chasing space pirates.

Although . . . I could've used his help right then. Anyone's help, actually. I was using one of the Meshenitai sims to do a little training of my own. Not that I needed it, but the the Royal Trials were days away, and I'd just learned it was going to be a Trios format. Three teammates.

I'd just gotten used to having *one* partner, and now I had to have two! Hopefully the Ibis and Fatima would get up to speed quickly. I'd assumed they'd want to join my team. Why wouldn't they? Two Meshenitai (well, one Meshenitai and one new recruit) plus me, the greatest gamer that ever crossed the stars? We couldn't lose! Good thing I scheduled an impromptu training session and messaged them about it in the middle of the night. They hadn't responded yet, which was weird, but maybe they were just too excited and stayed up all night watching the Royal Trials level reveal like I did. Now I just had to wait until they showed up and we could start training.

After they rescued me.

I sighed. I'd been doing fine! But apparently the Meshenitai training sims weren't configured with the latest patches from, well, any game played in the last century. Let alone the new Royal Trials levels. So I took the liberty of uploading them, tweaking them a bit to provide more of a challenge, and here we were! The perfect training sim!

Well, at least until the desert level glitched around me. My nefasi was just about to respond to the new level pick-ups (I added a turbo boost for fun) when, all of a sudden, the sim froze.

I couldn't move. I could only stare at the wonderfully rendered environment—the sandstorm threatening to engulf me was delightful—as I waited to be rescued. But any moment now the Ibis or Fatima or even Besa, my bionic mouse catcher/lioness/Guardian, would arrive and—

"Selam, my prince!" a cheerful voice said behind me.

I sighed. Maybe being rescued was overrated. "About time, Doombot."

A silver pyramid-shaped bot buzzed into my upside-down view. Gold lines swept diagonally down and around its surface, and the faint blue glow of its antigrav thrusters gave it a majestic look. Too bad it was just a glorified snitch.

"I'm glad the Azaj sent me to you," Doombot said. I named my REAR that as a joke, but since I always happened to get in trouble whenever it popped up, the name stuck. "According to my logs, it appears you have avoided my carefully laid schedule for today's events. I am here to rectify that."

"Can't help you there, Doombot. I'm super busy."

Doombot bobbed in the air and waited. Silence fell. I folded my arms and tried to whistle, but have you ever tried to whistle upside down? It's impossible. Just a few spluttering raspberries and a glob of drool. And you never want to drool while upside down.

After several seconds passed, Doombot spun in a circle. "Are you still—"

"Still busy!" I said, wiping my face. "My friends should be here any minute."

"Ah! If you are referring to the newest Meshenitai recruit—"

"The Ibis." I nodded.

"—and her trainer—"

"Fatima, too."

"—and your Guardian—"

"Besa, yep, those are the friends. They'll be here any minute now. Practice, you know?"

"—they're not coming."

"The Royal Trials are coming up soon, and Trios will be the toughest competition . . . Wait, what?" I glared at Doombot. "What do you mean, they're not coming? We've got practice! And I was up until morning programming this desert environment."

The helper bot spun on its axis again. "The human 'friends,' as you like to call them, have an assembly they're attending. Your lioness is being refit for close-quarters protection. Which leaves you, Your Highness. And as your schedule clearly says, this time was reserved for speech rehearsal."

I stared at it in confusion.

"For the upcoming Intergalactic Union reception?" Doombot said helpfully.

Still nothing.

"You have to give a speech about Axum's mission to find the missing modules."

My eyes widened. "Ooohhh, that! I thought that was, like, you know, optional."

"I'm afraid not, my prince. You will be required to stand in front of thousands of ambassadors, millions more watching via holofeed, and deliver a perfect speech that will surely be replayed around the galaxy far into the future. History will be made when you address the IU. Now, then, let's just go over . . . Wait, what are you doing? My prince?"

Look, I'm not afraid to admit I panicked here. But do you blame me? They wanted me to give a speech! To people! You send a princely message to the Nexus *one* time—in order to stop a rampaging Bulgu—and all of a sudden they make a figurehead out of you. Well, not this kid.

I unclipped the harness on my nefasi. "I don't do speeches. Nope. No, sirree, bot. I'm out. If anyone needs me, I'll be under my bed."

"But, my prince!"

"Later, Doombot," I called as the last snap unbuckled . . .

. . . and I began to fall six stories to the sim floor below.

The air whistled past my ears as I plummeted. Somewhere above me, I heard alarms blaring and Doombot shouting for help, but it all faded into the background as I squinted and let out a giant whoop.

"This is amaaaaaaaaaaaazing!" I shouted.

Everything merged together into a gray blur. The only thing that mattered was this moment. Me and the wind— artificial or not—between my fingertips as I spread my arms wide. I hadn't been able to get away from my newfound princely responsibilities for a while. Everyone wanted me to do something. Study the history of Axum. My family's history. Aunts and uncles and cousins and grandparents: this branch of the family tree or that one. Or maybe they, like Doombot, wanted me to do what princes were supposed to do. Make speeches, attend dinners, pose for holosims that would be broadcast throughout the galaxy.

And that's cool and all.

But . . .

What about me? Did being a prince mean I had to stop being Yared?

The grin faded as I scowled, my eyes still closed. No. Not today. Today, Yared was doing something I always wanted to do . . . fly.

I opened my eyes and flicked my wrist. A beam of light shot out from the sleeve of my flight suit, and I caught it in my left hand. Glanced down.

The sim floor grew closer and closer, much quicker than I'd expected.

I stretched the light out with the gleaming silver-etched black gloves on both my hands. The beam flattened into a wide, winged triangular shape that glowed brighter than a thousand stars.

The floor was only a dozen meters away.

I pushed the winged light toward my boots and kicked my heels into place, smirking when the energy board turned silver-blue. Birhani activation complete.

The floor was close enough for me to see my reflection, less than a meter before Axum's newest prince turned into Yared injera, when I twisted my legs sharply. The birhani pivoted, skated along the training room's wall, and let out a high whine as I grabbed the front lip of the energy board and shot forward, centimeters above the ground. I sped out of the room and into a curved hallway.

What? You thought I was in danger? Please.

I raced down the empty corridor, laughing and shouting. Sometimes I'd ride up one curved wall and loop around to the other side, dodging parked people movers and leaping over the occasional cleaner bot. The training sim room was located in one of the sections of Axum where no one had been for years, which was good and bad. It was good because it meant I could do whatever I wanted without someone telling me I was doing it wrong or wasn't doing it princely enough.

The bad? Well . . .

I swerved gently to avoid a stuffed undertaker bird lying in the middle of the corridor. Frowned, then began to slow.

Some child had probably dropped it and cried about missing it for weeks on end. Every now and then, no matter how hard I tried, I couldn't escape the knowledge that the Werari and their monster, the Bulgu, had done this. They forced the people of Axum to flee! To scatter across the galaxy! My heart broke all over again.

But that was the whole point of the journey we were on right now. Axum—the Emperor and Empress, their Meshenitai, Guardians, and other staff—was on its way to reunite the fractured pieces into a whole. Somewhere out there among the stars, a kid like me stared up and wondered where they really belonged.

I hoped we could bring them that answer soon.

To that end, we would need the help of others. Like the Intergalactic Union, or IU for short. The governing body of the galaxy. The people I had to make a speech in front of later.

I sighed, then paused and looked around. I . . . didn't recognize a single centimeter of my surroundings.

"Not again," I groaned. The one drawback to zooming around the abandoned sections of a giant space station: It was super easy to get lost.

A blue light flickered over my wrists as I opened my wrist comm. A map of the local area floated in the air in front of me. Scratching my head, I tried to zoom in and rotate to find out where I was, but the maze of passageways and doors made no sense. As I zoomed out to try and get a better look, a red light blinked on my wrist comm.

Message ping. Sender, Uncle Moti.

"Great," I said. "Just great. Just what I need, a lecture about getting lost and responsibilities and blah blah blah." I hesitated, then dismissed the alert. It was probably best for me to figure out where I was before facing the interrogation.

The birhani cast a soft glow as I floated in the middle of a giant six-way junction. Empty streets lined with benches and hoverlamps stretched off into the distance all around me. The space station was a giant obelisk surrounded by habitation rings larger than the city of Addis Prime, where I grew up, and it was far bigger on the inside. I got lost once trying to find a shower in my bedroom. (Fun fact: The showers were giant spheres that rotated around you, like standing in a gentle whirlpool that cleaned you instead of terrifying you.)

Anyhoo, traveling on a path toward the outer ring was called moving ringward, while traveling toward the inner ring, in the direction of the central obelisk, was called moving inward. From the little info I could pull from the map, I was in a section of the space station highlighted in orange, a flashing rectangular message in the middle.

"'Closed due to insufficient number of residents,'" I read aloud. "'Royal decree required to reopen.'"

I looked around. The highlighted section of the map was right in front of me. The streets were clear. The residential living modules, bright and airy hexagons with built-in green spaces, were in pristine condition. Somewhere in the distance, I could hear a water fountain, and hidden speakers filled the air with gentle birdsong.

Basically . . . it was perfect. And yet . . .

I sent the birhani humming down the street and drifted lazily from side to side, taking in the beautiful patterns and intricate designs decorating the sides of the lot of buildings. Holo-ads for neighborhood businesses, eateries, and other attractions materialized as I floated by. Street names written in Ge'ez traced themselves in light, disappearing as I moved on. I could almost hear the people going about their day—looking for a meal, gathering with friends, laughing at something that happened earlier in the day. It was . . . really sad.

Something beeped shrilly in the distance.

I froze.

What was that noise? I leaned forward, and the lightwing hummed a little faster down the street. "Hello?" I called out. "Anyone there?"

Nothing. Only the artificial birdsong. I frowned, then

sent the lightwing creeping forward even farther before coming to a stop near a plain one-story storage building. I listened for that weird noise, but there was nothing. The storage building's hatchway had lights running around it, but when I moved closer, it remained shut. Must've been locked.

The beeping sounded again. It was *definitely* coming from the storage building.

"I'm warning you, I have a"—I glanced down, then gulped—"a map, and I'm not afraid to use it."

Still no answer. I cruised forward a few more meters before frowning and slowing to a stop. Maybe I was just paranoid. Battling the Werari—had that really only been a few months ago?—had turned my nerves to glass. The slightest surprise would—

The floor beneath me fell away. A square section collapsed into a ramp that slid into darkness. I shouted as the birhani and I tumbled down, head over heels. I crashed into two poles, ribs first, and grunted in pain. That was going to leave a mark.

"Jeeez," I groaned, clutching my side. "I'm suing. Someone. Everyone. Who leaves a trapdoor there? That's just . . ."

My voice trailed off as the birhani—which had gone dark—flickered back to life. The light from the lightboard filled the room I'd just fallen into. I hadn't crashed into poles. They were legs. Armored legs. I stood slowly, the birhani rising with me.

Dented armor legs.

An armored chestplate that looked to be scorched and beat up beyond repair.

Midnight-black helmet with tinted faceshield.

"An exo," I whispered. "Old, but . . ."

A light blinked on in the upper-right corner of the faceshield . . . and the helmet moved.

I screamed and ran. I've never climbed anything as fast as I climbed that ramp. When I reached the top, I threw the birhani beneath my boots and cranked up the speed as far as it could go, only for it to flicker off again. It crashed to the street and sent me skidding across the ground once more.

Boots dropped into view as I rolled over. When I looked up, a group of silver-and-black Meshenitai exos, loaded down with a small armory, dropped to the ground in bright trails of fire. Five, ten, fifteen of them landed around me, circling in a ring of bristling metal and burning thrusters. Black faceshields masked them, and as one they unsheathed curved swords bigger than me, their blades rippling with black fire.

A bead of sweat rolled down my face. The birhani fizzled and disappeared.

"Um . . . hi?" I said.

One of the exos stepped forward, and the faceshield slid up.

"You are in huge trouble," said the Ibis.

CHAPTER TWO

Here are a couple of fun facts that I didn't know, and that I think could be helpful to future princes during their princely orientation:

1. Ditching your bodyguards is really frowned upon.

2. If you do decide to ditch them, make sure to disable the medallion you're wearing. It doubles as a homing beacon for your half-ton, heavily armored, diranium-clawed babysitter.

3. Especially if said medallion also recently had a mortifying, embarrassing, I'm-never-showing-my-face-in-public-again security upgrade installed.

"Seriously . . ." I said, shielding my eyes from the trio of holograms the medallion projected around me. Alarms blared, and a miniature floodlight appeared out of nowhere and blinked on and off. "Is all of this really necessary?"

The Ibis ignored me and kept walking. Three Meshenitai walked in front of us, and two more brought up the rear.

The corridors of Harar Station were decorated for Enkutatash; it was my first New Year's celebration away from Addis Prime. Back home (I had to stop thinking of Addis Prime as home; the station was my home now), the streets would practically be painted yellow as everyone hung daisies everywhere. There'd be singing and dancing, and school would be canceled. I was kind of homesick.

Here, holograms of daisies bloomed as we walked through hatchways before fading away behind us. There was also a group of Azmari-engineers who'd joined the station. The praise-singers were prized for their ability to design incredible holoscapes as they sang, and apparently they were pretty decent inventors as well. Uncle Moti told me they used to travel the galaxy, singing the story of the empire while using their skills to improve it. Pretty neat.

We moved quickly through imperial corridors decorated with floating portraits of triumphant moments in Axum history. Emperors and empresses welcoming new nations and peoples into Axum. The finished construction of a new spaceship. Me, being born.

"I was a wrinkly thing, wasn't I?" I asked, pausing and

squinting at the portrait. "Let me take a minute to study it. It's not every day you get to see a baby picture for the first time."

The Ibis rolled her eyes as she glanced back at me. "Just look in the mirror. Now stop stalling."

I stamped my feet. "I am *not* a baby. I just don't want everyone to see *this*." I gestured at the holograms standing next to me, and the Ibis's lips quirked, though she kept a serious expression on her face.

"Tough teff, Your Royal Irritation. Only three people can disable that feature, and two of them—your parents—are in a council meeting. That leaves the general as the only one who can shut it off. And if we don't, every Axumite ship in the galaxy will get a distress signal saying the prince is in danger, ordering them to return to his side at once. They won't be happy when they jump in-system only to find you triggered it by trying to—and I can't believe I'm repeating this—'escape from a mysterious and terrifying exo.' So stop throwing a tantrum."

"I am not throwing a tantrum!" I shouted. "It was *too* terrifying." The Ibis raised an eyebrow, and I groaned. "Fine. Whatever. Let's just get this over with."

"I'm not complaining too much," she said, savoring the moment. "On the one hand, you're in trouble, and on the other, it saves me from going back to scrapper dispersal. I swear, those bots make hives in the most inconvenient locations. And they mess up the astrogation data! It's such a hassle."

Scrappers were a type of bot that had been recently recognized as sentient AI, so they were on the same level as humans in terms of rights and privileges. Which was cool, except they liked to make assembly hives near communication antennae—basically nests for building more cute, terrifying scrapper bot babies. And the assembly hives wreaked havoc on comm signals. They were like giant bugs whose nests created dead zones. So annoying.

Almost as annoying as my medallion's security upgrade.

Beside me, three identical holographic displays of my mother, the Empress of Axum, followed me, hands cupped around their mouths, shouting at the top of their lungs for everyone in a light-year radius to hear. I'd muted the volume earlier, and now I unmuted just to see if the message had changed.

"OH, LISTEN! MY SON, THE PRINCE LIJ YARED, IS IN TROUBLE. THIS ONE, THIS BOY, THIS CHILD OF MINE NEEDS HELP. OH, LISTEN—"

I quickly muted it again.

The Ibis smirked as she waved her hand in front of the identification sensor on the circular door. It led to one of the station's many meeting rooms. Inside, Uncle Moti was in mid-conversation with another man I didn't recognize. I swear, adults had meetings like they needed them to survive. Food, oxygen, water, and meetings. The four elements of life.

"In you go, Lij Yared," the Ibis sang while bowing.

I glared at her. "Enjoy your scrapper relocation."

She stuck her tongue out, and I made a face at her until the hatch door spiraled shut. I sighed and walked deeper into the room. Soft lighting lit the interior, and music came from hidden speakers somewhere up on the cream-colored walls. I could smell something sizzling, and I realized the tables doubled as miniature buffet displays, piles of folded injera covering serving platters heaped with savory wot, tibs, and even shiro. The smell of the chickpeas bubbling with cubes of beef had me drooling.

And then there were the pyramids of flaky sambusas just waiting for the right boy to come along and stuff seven of them in his mouth. Me. I was that boy. I was on my way to perform my sacred duty that all tween-aged children are responsible for (namely, eating anything not nailed down) when Uncle Moti cleared his throat.

"Yared, over here, please."

I stopped mid-drool, looked at him, then glanced at the food, then looked back at Uncle Moti. He raised an eyebrow, and I sighed. Duty had to wait.

The three holograms of my mother marched over to where Uncle Moti and the strange man sat around the floating table of food. Five adults—and three of them weren't even real!—folded their arms and stared at me with the Look. The one where grown-ups haven't asked a question or accused you of anything, but they wait to see if you're going to tell on yourself. Which . . . come on. I haven't snitched on anyone in ten years. What makes you think I was gonna start doing it now, especially on MYSELF?

But the last thing I expected was for the strange man to stand up, clap both hands together, and smile at me. "Shall we get started?" he asked.

I looked at Uncle Moti, who also stood and walked over. He gently lifted the medallion from around my neck and spoke into it.

"General Moti Berihun," he said, and the holograms disappeared. I squinted in confusion. Yes, I was happy my mother was no longer following me and wailing in triplicate. But the last time Uncle Moti had brought me to one of his meetings without any warning, it was before I even knew the Werari and Axum existed. He'd sold the magnetic soles of our grav-boots to a scrap-collecting drone, in exchange for two huge refrigerated containers of niter kibbeh. Uncle Moti loved putting pats of the spiced butter in his morning coffee, but we couldn't reach the top floor of our warehouse apartment for a month.

(He also sold the ladders that we used to climb up there for a hovering chopping board he could use to prepare wot.)

(Times were tough.)

"What's going on?" I asked suspiciously. "I left my grav-boots back in my room."

"Oh, by the stars, boy, that was one time," Uncle Moti said, his face flushing. "And you used the butter just as much as I did."

"Because that was the only thing in the fridge. Butter. Breakfast, lunch, dinner. If I wanted a snack—butter."

We would've continued arguing, except the third man in the room raised his hands. The lights in the room brightened, then dimmed, and the hovering table floated up into a hidden door in the ceiling. A two-dimensional display appeared around his wrist, a transparent green circle divided into sections. He studied them, then flicked his wrist, and the display rotated. A section highlighted, and I gasped as the man's clothes changed colors before my eyes. Where before he'd been wearing a white shamma over cream pants and a tunic, now his whole outfit was white trimmed in dazzling gold.

"How did you do that?" I asked, stepping forward to

examine the display. It was like something out of a video game. An item wheel, that's what they were called.

"Introductions first, my prince." The man bowed so low his beard brushed the polished floor, and he spoke in a flowing rhythm, like he was reciting poetry. "I, Lij Yared, honored Dejazmach Moti Berihun, am an Azmari. I am honored to be here—"

"Dejazmach?" I whispered.

"Commander of the army," Uncle Moti whispered back.

"Oh, I thought it meant butter buyer."

His eyes flashed, but he smothered a smile as the man continued.

"I am here to transfer this Radial system to you. As you've no doubt been briefed, the process should be seamless and quick. You'll be able to pass through security checkpoints and interact with any station AI once we're done here. Your Radial will unlock it all. It is a rite of passage for royal heirs, a symbolic bestowal of the keys granted to them in accordance with their growing role in intergalactic affairs."

I tried to keep my face still at the mention of the briefing. Right. I knew I'd forgotten something. I could literally feel Uncle Moti's gaze on the back of my head, but if I turned around now, he'd know I missed the briefing. He would probably cancel the ceremony.

Plus . . . who didn't want cool new technology that could

get them through any security checkpoint? So I stared at the Azmari and tried to nod in all the right places as the man explained how it worked.

"Each Radial system is handcrafted by an Azmari-engineer. Tiny nanites build the interface as we praise-singers tell stories of the intended wearer. Their history, their favorite food, their mistakes—the nanites craft a Radial that is specially designed and one of a kind. The Radial is presented to its new owner on the eve of their twelfth birthday, welcoming them as a warrior and protector of Axum. A leader! A prince!"

At some point, the Azmari's explanation had switched cadences, growing from words into song. An instrument materialized in his hands. It was a single-stringed violin-like device; the Azmari played it with a curved bow made of light. Uncle Moti sat down to one side of him and began to clap his hands softly in rhythm.

"A prince!" the Azmari repeated. "Returned to us as Axum returns to the skies from whence she first ascended. A prince! Building the future. Carrying the past. History's dream and the present's inspiration. A prince!"

I stood in utter amazement as the Radial system began to expand around the Azmari, growing and separating into sections of light. Bright blue with streaks of silver, it began to float over to me as the Azmari sang. Then it settled over my left and right arms, piece by piece—just above the hands, then the wrists and forearms, and then just beneath the elbows. Spinning discs of light assembled themselves around my arms. Silver lines separated them into sections. Many of them were blank, but a few had pictures and words on them.

I only realized the Azmari had stopped when Uncle Moti cleared his throat. "Thank you," I hurried to say. "But . . . um, what do they do?"

Uncle Moti sighed. "Did you read *any* of my briefing?"

"Some of it. The title, definitely. Maybe. I definitely thought about reading it. At some point."

The Azmari snorted. "It is normal for the system to take some time to adjust to its new wearer. Engage the Radial by flicking your wrists like so. They don't have to be engaged for identification, but they do have to be active to interact with technology such as exoskeletons or ship controls."

"Exos! It can control exos?"

The Azmarik nodded. "You can control and interact with any Axumite technology without restrictions. Or, you will, once the system has acclimated to you. You can run diagnostics at any time by asking it to. All commands can be initiated by saying, 'System, do this or do that.'"

"But it's not the eve of my birthday," I said, looking at Uncle Moti. "Why give this to me now?"

He shifted uncomfortably. "Call it a safety precaution. Only members of the Axum royal family receive Radials. There will be a lot of people trying to challenge you, or claim you aren't who you say you are. Some will doubt you no matter what, especially after you give your speech."

Right. The other thing I was dreading. My speech.

"The Radial is a way to prove them wrong, just in case I'm not there. And, I suppose, it'll help with your other early birthday present."

He laughed as I exploded out of my seat and peppered him with questions. "Not now," Uncle Moti said, motioning for me to sit back down. "I'll show you later. For the moment, I have to get you to your parents or we'll both be in trouble."

The Azmari picked up his instrument and bowed to Uncle Moti and me. "And I must depart as well, to prepare for this evening's performance. Lij Yared, honored Dejazmach, I hope you'll be able to attend. The Emperor and Empress themselves have requested me. I wish you safe travels on your journeys."

He turned to go, then paused and turned around. "A word of advice, young prince. The Radial can interface with *any* Axum technology, new or old. Be careful."

And with that, the Azmari praise-singer swept out of the room, leaving me with two fading wheels of light and a whole lot of questions. What other cool things could the Radial do? Was there an instruction manual? Could I order sambusas to go? These were questions that needed answering. But when I turned to Uncle Moti, he had a stern expression on his face.

"And now I think it's time to talk about the little . . . adventure you just had."

My face fell. Sometimes I felt like the universe was powered by never-ending lectures.

CHAPTER THREE

The Emperor and Empress of Axum sat on silver thrones surrounded by stars. Seriously. Planets, too. An entire solar system swirled around what was called the People's Chamber. They refused to call it a throne room. My mother once said they were representatives of the people.

When I'd asked Uncle Moti what that meant, he stood for a moment and thought about it, then pointed at the diagram of a ship he was reviewing for the Axum fleet.

"My boy," he said, "you can be one of two things as a leader. You can be a rocket, or you can be a shield." As he spoke, he tapped the different components of the ship respectively. "A rocket consumes energy and then blasts off. It sits behind the rest of the ship, letting the body of the vessel take the damage and protect it. It gets us where we need to go, but if you don't take precautions, the heat and energy can be destructive. Even deadly. But the shield . . . the shield lies at the front of the ship. It takes the brunt of the damage so the ship doesn't have to. Someday you will have to determine, as a leader, if you're going to let the people protect *you* or if you're going to protect the people.

The People's Chamber resembled the many other meeting rooms situated around the space station (again with the meetings). Diamond-shaped, vaulted ceilings, with a few ornamental aquaponic fountains full of fish and plants. There were two rows of workstations populated by different staff lined at the room's edges, one on either side, leaving a giant space for holodisplays like the one I currently marched through.

One by one, every face in the room turned toward me. I could feel the back of my neck grow warm in embarrassment, but I kept my eyes on the two rulers of Axum. Two pairs of eyes that had my shape and color. Noses like mine. Brows crinkled in mild irritation just like I— Wait. They were irritated.

The rulers of Axum.

My parents.

I would never get tired of saying that.

As if she read my thoughts, the Empress—my mother—smiled and shook her head, even as her eyes still crinkled with worry.

"And there he is. My son."

Did my chest puff out a little when I heard that? Yes.

Did it deflate a bit when Uncle Moti tousled my hair before heading off to his own workstation? Also yes. I spent ten minutes with the stylist-bot this morning! But fashion is a lifestyle, and not everyone gets that.

"Mother," I said, then looked at the Emperor. "Father."

My dad raised an eyebrow, then gestured toward Uncle Moti, whose workstation showed a holovid displaying a transparent blue-and-green planet with a single moon orbiting it. "Do you want to handle this? Or should I?"

"Hmm," said Uncle Moti. His demeanor changed slightly as he spoke. He was the leader of the Burning Legion of Axum, after all, the finest fighting force in the galaxy, and—as recently as three months ago—the man I only knew as Uncle Moti.

"I would, Your Majesty. But . . . actually, I think someone else would like to have a word."

I exhaled a little. Uncle Moti wasn't going to lecture me? Fine with me. I could handle discipline from anyone else. My uncle had a way of letting you know he was disappointed while also giving you a pep talk. Then at the end you're somehow offering to ground *yourself*. It was like magic. But if he was stepping aside, I was off the hook. The only person who could make me feel any worse wasn't a person, but a—

"Mrowr."

—bionic lioness.

A creature the size of a neo-rhino stalked out of the darkness behind Uncle Moti. Armor covered its flanks and legs, and spikes the size of my arm emerged from a ridge along the spine. Fangs like knives. Claws like sickles. The symbol of a roaring lion etched in the middle of its forehead.

"Hi, Besa," I said quietly.

Besa was my bionic lioness and Guardian, designed to be my bodyguard and protector after the first Werari invasion, before I was born. She alone knew where I was at all times, because of the medallion I wore that was synced to her programming. And from the low, rumbling growl threatening to fill the whole chamber, she was none too happy with me.

"Listen," I said. "I can explain."

Besa sat on her haunches and quirked an ear. Insolently, too, if I might add, but I let it slide.

"I was just doing some training," I said. "For the Royal Trials. The new Trios mode. But then the alert happened and I went exploring—"

"Mrowr."

"Yes, it wasn't a great time to go exploring, but I'm ready to give my speech—"

"Mrowr mrowr."

"No, it's . . . not exactly written yet. I thought I'd give an off-the-cuff, inspirational talk. Something motivating yet personal."

"Mrowr."

"Oh, wow, that's rude. I only did that one time, and that's because I drank too much spris and my stomach didn't agree with me."

Besa stood and began pacing around me, yowling like I was some sort of wet-behind-the-ears little kid. "Mrowr mrowr, mroworor mrowr. Mrowr!"

"Hey!" I said, pointing at her. "Watch the language."

"What I'm sure she means to say," Uncle Moti interrupted, "is that you are no longer just a boy running the streets of Addis Prime. You were never just a boy. You are a prince of Axum—you have certain responsibilities now."

"Like speeches," I grumbled.

A few of the others in attendance chuckled. I didn't see what was funny. Who liked giving speeches? All that talking, my mouth getting dry, and sometimes my palms started sweating more than Uncle Moti after eating a bowl of spicy yasa tibs. There. I said it. Old sweaty-palmed Yared. Happy?

Suddenly, the Emperor stood. Four Meshenitai instantly materialized at his side, bracketing him. "Your Highness?" one of them asked.

He waved them off. "I think," he said, "that we are being a bit harsh with my son. I knew I would be Emperor for two decades, with guides and mentors my whole life. He has had less than a year."

Uncle Moti nodded thoughtfully. My dad stepped forward and clapped him on the shoulder. "Let me take it from here," he said before turning to me. "Come with me, Yared. I have something to show you."

I followed him as he walked toward the chamber's exit, Meshenitai on either side. My ears burned. Great. Another lecture, this one from my father. How could this get any worse?

"Mrowr," Besa said, swiping at me as I went by. Have you ever had a souped-up rat trap smack you? It's not fun. I whirled around and glared at her, ready to retaliate, when the meaning of what she said registered in my mind.

"Grounded! What do you mean, grounded?"

"Mrowr."

"You! I . . . You can't . . . UGH!" I pointed at her, but words failed me. I turned and stomped out of the room. My mother's chuckle was the last thing I heard before the door hissed shut.

"So," I said, "I have a question."

The Emperor and I stood in an oval lift with lightscreens instead of walls. Streams of data swirled on them, circling around us, constantly updating and changing color status from green to orange to—in a few spots—bright flashing red.

My father studied a smaller cone of data hovering above his wrist comm. "Hmm? Oh, don't worry about this. You'll get your own daily briefs soon. It can be a bit overwhelming at first, but from what I gather and what General Berihun tells me, you'll have the hang of it in no time."

"Oh." I scanned the data cone more closely. It *did* look interesting. I could probably do some customization and feed in HKO leaderboards and—oh, and Royal Trials leader-boards, too! The thought of tweaking and skinning the interface kept me distracted for a few moments. Then I shook my head.

"No, I mean, that'd be awesome, but I wanted to ask something different."

"Oh?" The Emperor raised an eyebrow as he flicked a chunk of data to the lift wall. It expanded into a summary of the space station's progress.

"Yes. Um . . . what do I call you?"

The Emperor, my father, froze for just an instant before he turned his full gaze on me. His eyes narrowed, then soft-ened as he dropped to a knee. The cone of data disappeared and he reached a hand out to settle on my shoulder.

"What do you mean, my son?"

I fidgeted. "That's just it. You can call me son, which is easy. It's only one thing, you know? But . . . I don't know what you like to be called. Father? Dad? His Imperial Pop Pop?"

"Yared," my father said. "Son . . ."

But the words were pouring out now. "There's so much I haven't figured out yet, and it's like I'm standing in this elevator with data swirling around me and I don't know what it all means. Am I supposed to understand it, or will it be homework, or am I being silently judged by everybody because I don't automatically do the right thing? I'm just supposed to pick the right thing to do at the right moment and . . . what if I choose wrong? What if it's all wrong?"

Suddenly, I was swept into a giant hug. You know the kind—the one that makes you feel that the only important thing in that moment, in that space, is you.

"Dad," he said quietly.

"What?"

The Emperor pulled back and grinned. "Dad. You can call me Dad. His Imperial Pop Pop was your grandfather, may the stars guide his spirit."

I smiled back. "Okay . . . Dad."

Dad stood but kept his hand on my shoulder. The data cone reappeared, but this time he shunted the very bottom cross-section toward the lightscreen. It dissolved into a two-dimensional map of the space station, which faded away, module by module, until only the five massive Menelik drives remained. Tiny pinpricks of light swarmed around them, and I realized that those represented people. My ancestors? I was watching the space station getting built.

"I know it feels like a lot of information is being thrust at you at once," Dad said. He gestured at the Menelik drives. "Take it step by step. You must remember, Axum was not built in a day. Nor in a generation. It took time. Patience. The knowledge we gathered along the way was passed down to future generations. We made mistakes. We had setbacks."

One of the Menelik drives exploded, and I gasped. The entire structure collapsed, and Dad flicked the image away, a look of dismay on his face. "But we always took it one problem at a time, one day at time. We looked to the future. To the stars."

He tapped in a command to his wrist comm and flung his arms wide. The lightscreen went dark, then burst into brilliance with a giant exo standing in front of us.

"Did you know the first exos we built were not for our guards or warriors? They were for our builders so they might be protected from the dangers of building a space station as massive as our ancestors envisioned. They were built to smash meteors and mine comets. The pilots were not Meshenitai. Do you know who they were?"

I shook my head.

Dad dropped a hand on my shoulder again. "Us. Queens and kings of Axum. How could we ask of our people that which we would not do ourselves? Moti has a saying—be a shield, not a rocket. Being a prince, Yared, is not just about speeches, though they are important. Nor the wardrobe, although"—he brushed an imaginary speck of dust off his shoulder—"we do look good."

I snickered, and he winked before getting serious again. "But being a leader of Axum is about service. If you have privilege, if you have power, then you have a responsibility. And that, my son, is the first lesson you must learn. Responsibility for our actions."

"Like taking off without telling anyone," I said, sighing. I knew that would get tied into our conversation at some point. At least it *was* a conversation, not a straight-up lecture.

Dad nodded. "Exactly. There are people responsible for your safety, as there are for mine and your mother's. If something happened to you . . ."

He fell silent but squeezed my shoulder. I nodded. I was ready to ask more questions about my other princely duties.

Now that I had him here, I might as well get as much info out of him as I could. He was the Emperor of Axum . . . he had to have all the answers, right?

But the lift hummed to a stop at that moment, the door hissing open to reveal one of the most astonishing sights I'd ever seen.

"Where are we?" I whispered.

Dad smiled. "Incredible, isn't it? It's called the Walk of Sheba. When my father first showed me this place, I think I stayed up here two nights in a row. It is . . . something truly wonderful."

We stepped out onto a platform just wide enough for the two of us to walk side by side. It was made of some dark gray metal that glittered as I walked, leaving flowing footprints behind me. After about twenty or so meters, the platform widened into an oval with room for several people to stand. But it was what stretched out beyond that captivated me.

A lightscreen arched from my left, curving high overhead and dropping to my right in a single, seamless panel. As I stepped beneath it, holding my breath, stars winked into existence. Then planets. Satellites and comm buoys. Far, far in the distance, a space station floated in orbit.

"Is this a simulation?" I whispered.

Dad shook his head. "Thousands of sensors covering the exterior of our space station shunt data here, to give us a real-time approximation of the space in which we travel. What you are watching is our approach into the Sol-Luna System—our destination and the headquarters of the Intergalactic Union."

I grimaced at those last two words. The IU is where I'd have to give my speech. But even that couldn't dampen my spirits for long, not while I was standing here among the planets and star of a system I'd never been to before. My first voyage, not just as a prince but as . . . well, as Yared. I couldn't wait to see what—

Alarms went off. The view of the Sol-Luna System disappeared, replaced by an exterior shot of Harar Station. There was something familiar about that section of the space station, but what was obviously *not* supposed to be there was the transport ship currently trying to force its way onto a docking pad. It hovered next to the nonresponsive structure, then flipped around so it was pointed in the other direction, heading out toward one of the rings spinning around the station.

Dad's face tightened, and he whirled around. "Wait here for Moti," he ordered. Then he sprinted back to the lift, barking into his wrist comm for the Meshenitai we'd left at the bottom. The hatchway spiraled open, and before it closed, he tapped a command and the lift hatch went red. Lockdown. "Don't worry. You're safe," he said.

And then I was left alone.

My head was spinning. Everything had moved in a blur. Intruders? As soon as we'd arrived in-system? Were they the Werari? Or someone else? Whatever the case, I was safe as long as I remained here. Right?

No sooner had I thought that than the ship returned on-screen. It headed back toward the cargo docking pad, and this time—to my horror—the docking pad engaged, extending so the strange ship could land.

"That . . . can't be good," I said. I looked down at the Radial on my wrist, then copied the movements the Azmari-engineer had done, flicking my wrist so the circular interface appeared.

"System," I said, "identify that docking pad."

A voice not dissimilar to Azaj's sounded from the Radial. "Docking pad connected to abandoned residential section. Relevant schematic downloading—error, map already downloaded. Relevant area highlighted."

I opened the map and inhaled as I recognized the section. It was the area where I'd fallen through the floor. There weren't any Meshenitai there; they were all heading to the docking ring. I had to warn someone.

"Contact Uncle Moti," I said.

"Station-wide communications lockdown in effect until intruders are identified."

Of course. I hesitated, then looked at the map again. I knew where to go. I could get there and use the Radial to trigger an alarm again. The Meshenitai would come find me just like they did last time, and in force. I nodded. I had a plan.

I sprinted to the elevator and engaged the Radial. "System, unlock lift doors."

"Lij Yared Heywat recognized. Doors unlocked."

I grinned. This was going to be so useful. I entered the lift and spent the entire descent finding the fastest route to that abandoned area of Harar Station. I also requested some stun-drones to meet me there. I wasn't taking any chances.

When the lift opened, I was already on my birhani and speeding through the corridors. I cranked it up to full speed and leaned over the lightboard, swerving around obstacles and occasionally riding the walls to avoid slowing down. I had to hurry. I continued to try to contact someone, *anyone*, through my wrist comm and Radial, but apparently super-awesome security permissions didn't extend to a comms lockdown. Probably for the best. I didn't know what I would do if I had the power to contact anyone at any time, anywhere on the station. Probably pretend to be a ghost haunting Besa's tail.

I arrived at the junction outside the abandoned residence area just in the nick of time. Six stun-drones—flying dragon-like bots the size of my hand—appeared. The bots wrapped up their targets with their long tails to restrain them; a zap of electricity subdued other bots and potentially unruly people. The zaps were relatively harmless—don't ask me how I knew. (Okay, I tested one out on myself and ended up stuck for ten minutes on the floor of my closet. Don't tell anyone.)

The stun-drones landed on my arms like armored gauntlets, three on either side. I took a deep breath, then triggered the alarm on my medallion and cruised to a stop just as the hatch separating the junction from the residence area beyond hissed open.

"Stop right there!" I shouted. "You are trespassing on—"

I didn't finish my sentence. Could you blame me?

The largest bot I'd ever seen on a ship appeared. Eight legs, two vicious mandibles, and standing the size of a kebele bus, it stalked into the junction. Riding it was an almost-equally large person covered head to toe in ceremonial exo-armor. They also wore a matching oversized mask that resembled a smiling face. For some reason, it didn't put me at ease.

More spider-mechs appeared, but none quite as big as the first. A second person appeared in a black-and-silver suit with a beautiful silver mask shaped in the image of a crying man.

The first warrior leaned over the giant spider-mech. "Get . . ." their low voice growled from behind the mask, "*out* of our way."

CHAPTER FOUR

The exo-warrior on the spider-mech lifted something from their back—a giant ax, the largest I'd ever seen—and pointed it at me. They didn't speak again. Not that I could have heard them if they did. The station's alarms were shrieking, drowning out whatever identification the intruder would've offered.

If they would've offered any. From the way the ax was pointed unwaveringly at me, we might've moved beyond pleasantries.

They shifted on the giant spider-mech—which snapped its sharp metal mandibles at me. Each of its eight legs shimmered from the exhaust of their thrusters. It was the size of a horse and as wide as a hoverbus. But it was also old. Dents and cracks covered most of its armor. What had to have been once-brilliant black, emerald green, and silver paint now looked faded and dull. But old or not, it was still dangerous. I had to hold them here until Uncle Moti or the Meshenitai arrived.

The spider-mech hissed at me and stepped forward.

"Spiders," I muttered to myself. "Why does everyone have to have spiders?"

Suddenly, the alarms cut off. I breathed a sigh of relief—help had arrived. But then a flash of movement grabbed my attention. The slim spider-mech moved in front of the giant, and the rider touched off their mask in a mocking salute. Their hands were brown, and they had to be young, maybe even my age. They were shaved bald except for two thin braids hanging from their left temple and curling over their shoulder—a younger style, one I hadn't seen anyone on the station with.

"We are looking for the Negus and Negiste," they shouted. "Can you inform them—"

"Who are you?" I interrupted.

"Excuse me?"

"Whatever it is you think you're about to do, think again." I slid a stun-drone down my arm and held it in front of me. "You can't just break in and start issuing demands. One, that's rude, and two . . . well, really there's only one, but pretend I said something profound and amazing here."

The figure opened their mouth to respond, but at that moment, the giant spider-mech let out a horrifying hiss. The huge figure in the armored exo swung one leg over and hopped down from their mount. I instantly launched two stun-drones into the air. They circled above my head, ready to strike if I instructed them to.

"Let us pass," came a deep, growling voice from the tinted helmet. "I will not ask again."

"No," I said.

"Do you know who I am?"

My fingers tightened on the drone controls. They buzzed within striking distance of the giant. I was proud of the way my voice didn't waver as I raised an eyebrow. "No. Should I?"

The ax swirled through the air in a tight circle, then lashed out, clipping the drones and sending them clattering to the floor. My jaw dropped. How was that even possible? I quickly sent two more at them, but the spider-mech swatted them out of the air with two of its legs.

"Step out of the shadows," the giant roared.

I gulped, then checked my wrist comm. No one had told me they were on their way, but I had to keep the intruders here until someone eventually showed up. I could stall until then. I'd made bigger bluffs . . . I think.

I stepped forward, my last two stun-drones buzzing above my shoulder. "Visiting hours are over," I said. "If you want to leave a message, I'll be sure to tell somebody at some point. If I feel like it."

The spider-mech hissed. The armored giant stepped

forward, and my fingers tightened on the drone controls. Just a bit longer.

"You insolent jackal," the giant said. "I should have you flattened and pressed into a mold to hang from my wall. I've wiped more respectful trash off the bottom of my boots."

"First off, ew. Secondly, you are the intruder. You want to talk about respect? Who breaks into someone else's home and starts lecturing them on respect?"

"Enough!" The spider-mech reared and screeched a challenge as the giant's battle-ax swung in circles above their head. I was absolutely sure the entire gang of spider-mechs and their exo riders were going to charge. I grimaced. No help had arrived. Did I need to set off my Mom-in-triplicate alarm to get saved around here? I guess it was up to me. No one was going to attack my home again, not while I could still fight. The stun-drones flew forward, searching for an opening.

"I am Balamba Ras!" the giant shouted, ripping off his mask. "And I will speak with my uncle." I got the briefest glimpse of a wide-faced man with a massive beard before, to my horror, the huge spider-mech charged and the giant barreled after it.

Wait, uncle? Hold on a second . . .

Suddenly, every single light in the docking area turned on. Spotlights, emergency lights, warning lights, all of them. In the middle of the pandemonium, the giant, Balamba Ras, and his mech skidded to a stop. An enormous hologram materialized between them and me, and I let out a sigh of relief. It was the virtual palace minister, Azaj.

"Perhaps I can be of service," Azaj boomed in his calm yet mildly annoyed tone. It was the voice the AI always used when I was on the verge of making a terrible mistake.

But when both of the intruders bowed to the AI, I got a sinking feeling in the pit of my stomach that told me this time I might have actually messed up.

"Honored Azaj of the Emperor," the younger man said, rising from his bow and holding a fist over his heart. "We, servants of the Empire, seek an audience with the Negus and Negiste."

Azaj bowed back, shrinking down to normal size now that there were no battle-axes or spider-mechs threatening me.

"Of course, Mesfina. Right away. The Emperor and Empress are"—did the AI glance at me?—"expecting you."

Oh. Wow. Now I felt ridiculous.

But not as ridiculous as the feeling that washed over me when Azaj turned toward the still-fuming giant, his armored helmet now removed and tucked under his arm.

"And welcome to you as well, Balamba Ras. Might I introduce you to the Royal Heir, Lij Yared the First, Prince of Axum? And, if I might add . . . your cousin."

Balamba Ras's booming laughter echoed around the huge dining room. The other, younger man—who I found out wasn't related to me but was just as important as my cousin—was named Mesfina. They, along with my parents and Uncle Moti and several other ministers and officials, all gathered around the giant circular briefing table. I stared glumly at the plate of wot and injera in front of me. Normally it was my favorite, and the chef had even given me an extra portion of the spicy dish. But my appetite had disappeared, along with my chances of going to watch the Royal Trials. I had goofed up. Bad.

"And then he had the nerve to challenge me to a wrestling match! Me! Three times his size and five years older." Balamba Ras threw back his head and laughed again. He and Mesfina had removed their armor and now wore shamma flight suits like everyone else. Except instead of the obelisk patches, they each had a golden flat-topped mountain with several stars floating around it. Mesfina still wore his mask, which was confusing, but no one else seemed to question it. While my father and Mesfina argued over who had actually won the wrestling match that Balamba Ras and Dad participated in when they were children, I leaned over and asked Uncle Moti about the patches.

He rubbed his beard and swirled the small cup of tej he held in his right hand. "That? It represents the *Amba*. Centuries ago, when we were still land-bound on Old Earth, ambas were high mountains with flat tops, perfect for strategic positioning. When Axum took to the stars, we kept the term as a reminder of home and bestowed it upon the technology that would allow us to always protect the planet we left. The *Amba* is . . . well, it was one of the most important pieces of technology Axum had, before the Werari destroyed it."

Uncle Moti took a sip of his tej and nodded at Balamba Ras. "He governed it. Hence his title of Bal*amba* Ras."

I frowned. "Wait, that isn't his name? I was calling him Cousin Ras!"

Uncle Moti chuckled. "Balamba Ras is a title, as is Ras itself. So is Mesfina, for that matter. They are bestowed upon worthy protectors of Axum by the Emperor and Empress, as both an honor and a request: that they should become servants of the people."

I glanced at the swirling designs on Mesfina's mask. "Is keeping his face covered a part of the job?"

Mesfina chuckled. He turned toward me and gave a slight bow, the mask glinting in the light of the lamps hovering above the briefing table. I flushed. I didn't know my voice had carried that far. But he simply raised his glass to me. There was a friendly, mocking note in the buzzing voice coming through the helmet speakers as he leaned forward.

"The helmet, unfortunately, is my own doing, Lij Yared. A vow I have taken. Until Adwa is restored to Axum and I lay eyes upon her glory, no one will lay eyes upon my face. The warriors who follow me take the same vow, though it is not required."

"Sweaty and uncomfortable," Balamba Ras grunted.

"Perhaps, but it is about more than comfort. It is about what is right. About justice."

I nodded. That I could understand. I may have been new to being a prince and everything that came with it, but keeping a vow was basically like keeping a promise. Mesfina was promising to fight for Adwa. It was a responsibility that he'd placed on himself. For his people and everyone who followed him. Like what a prince was supposed to do. Now I just had to figure out what, exactly, Adwa was.

"I'll help, too," I said suddenly. "With Adwa. Whatever I can do, I'll do it."

"That's my son," my mother said, beaming.

"So," I began, trying to keep everything straight in my head. It wasn't going well. "What's an Adwa?"

Balamba Ras, who was in the middle of taking a sip of tej, spluttered. "What have you been teaching the boy, Berihun?" he called across the table. Apparently, our conversation had reached everyone's ears. Great.

"How to survive, my friend," Uncle Moti said softly. "How to survive."

Balamba Ras grunted and waved off the remark, then turned to me. "Adwa, Prince, was . . . *is* the astrolabe in the stars. The compass for space travel." He pounded the table and leaned back in his seat. "A technological marvel, handicapped by bureaucracy."

Mesfina tapped a finger. "To be more helpful, Adwa used to be a part of this very space station. It sat right below Harar Station, if I'm not mistaken. It helped us navigate: a giant, constantly updating astrolabe. Ships could use it to update their own charts. Without it, space travel would be a series of guesses."

Something about that didn't make sense to me. When I looked up, Uncle Moti and Dad were smiling, as if they already knew what I was going to ask.

"But I thought the Menelik drives helped us travel?"

Uncle Moti shook his head gently. "Think of Adwa and the Menelik drives as two parts of a whole, working together to get us where we need to go. The Menelik drives will take you there, and quickly, but before that you have to figure out a safe route. That's where Adwa comes in."

"A giant astrolabe," I repeated in disbelief.

"It used to be protected by the *Amba*," Mom said. "But

when the Werari destroyed the fortress, the resulting explosion blew out nearly all the sensors and satellites in the quadrant. By the time we could send a rescue party, all traces of the facility had vanished. And with the Werari chasing us, we didn't have time to search properly. We could only leave automated life-pods to rescue the survivors and lead the Werari away."

"My life was saved by one of those pods," Mesfina murmured. The mask lifted, and the eyes behind it stared at me. "Those of us . . . left behind on Old Earth were fortunate enough to scrabble together an existence, building a community out of the rubble. The IU helped where it could, but we've only just reached pre-Werari levels. And now it looks like even that little bit of progress is in jeopardy."

I raised my eyebrows. "Why?"

Balamba Ras slammed his fist down on the table again, and several ministers jumped. He scowled. "Because trouble is stirring down on Old Earth. And we need to be prepared. Which is why we're here. Let us get down to business."

Mom nodded, and everyone straightened in their seats. She stood, activating the briefing table with a wave of her own Radial. The lights in the room dimmed, and a hologram of Old Earth materialized above the table. I groaned. Uncle Moti elbowed me. I just . . . I thought I'd *escaped* a lecture.

"Old Earth and her orbital traffic," she said.

The planet where people first took to the stars loomed above us all, blue and green and brown, like an emerald covered in dust. Above its surface, satellites circled, ships launched into the atmosphere or descended to the planet, and two gigantic space stations orbited slowly like moons. The first station I recognized from history holovids. Old Earth's International Space Station was the model all other nations and empires used for their own technological palaces in the sky.

The other space station dwarfed the ISS—and *that* was our current destination. The *Benevolence*, home of the Intergalactic Union, and where we would warn everyone about the threat of the Werari.

But there were more objects floating around the planet. Many more. If I didn't know any better, I'd say it was an asteroid field or a planetary ring. Except Old Earth didn't have any of those. So that meant . . .

"Is that space junk?" I blurted out.

Mom stopped her briefing, and everyone turned to look at me. I winced. Right. There were more important things to talk about. But she nodded as if I'd made a good point. "Precisely. Thank you, Yared. Old Earth's orbit is a hazardous maze of old satellites, damaged ships, broken comm relays, and even bubble shelters."

She must've seen my confused expression because Mom added, "Those are pods where people set up living spaces that they've cobbled together."

"People live there?!" I couldn't believe it. It looked incredibly dangerous. How did they get food or water or oxygen supplies?

"Not just people, pirates!" Balamba Ras shouted, banging the briefing table so hard the hologram of Old Earth flickered.

"Come, now—" Mesfina began, placing an arm on the giant man's shoulder. But Balamba Ras shook it off, and Mesfina sighed and sat back. He noticed me watching and shrugged, as if this was a recurring event with the giant man.

"Those floating death traps are a haven for the pirates who raid our farms and facilities on Old Earth. Impossible to patrol. We've tried, and the devious little scavengers just disappear like insects into the walls. Any ship that tries to pass through to Old Earth that isn't a battleship finds itself under attack. The wretched vermin are well armed, too. A regular space militia. Even the *Amba* would have had a tough time dealing with them." The man grimaced. I guess the memory of his former command was a constant sore spot for him. "Thankfully they restrict their activities to Old Earth. But you'll face some trouble getting to the

Benevolence. At least a squadron or two." Balamba Ras sat back and nodded at the Emperor. "That's why I'm glad you finally saw the sense in my suggestion, Negus. The young prince will appreciate the time to study, be reflective, and finally learn something."

Now I was so engrossed in how the Radial system interacted with the briefing table that I almost missed those last two sentences. Glowing miniature replicas of beat-up ships puttered around a tiny debris town that hovered above my wrist. From my vantage point, they didn't look like pirates. Actually, it looked like any other woreda back on Axum Prime—people going about their business while trying to scratch out a living. But maybe that's what pirates wanted you to think. Balamba Ras had been here longer than me. He had to know better, right?

Wait.

What did he say?

I looked up to see everyone watching me. Every adult had that expression on their face. You know the one. Where a decision was made and it was For the Best* and they were waiting on you to realize it and not make a scene.

(*according to their superior grown-up logic)

My name is Yared TheGr8. Prince or no prince, making scenes is what I do.

I inhaled, held it, then let it all out in a burst. "WHAT?"

"Yared . . ." Uncle Moti began, but I looked at Mom.

"What does 'time to study and be reflective' mean? What am I reflecting? Light? That's just scientifically unsound."

"Mrowr."

Besa's tail lashed my knee, but I ignored her reprimand as well. I wasn't going to let a cat who'd gotten banned from Harar Station's loading docks because she couldn't stop chasing the guidance lasers tell me how to behave.

"I thought we were going to the opening ceremonies for the Royal Trials." I hated how there was a hint of a whine in my voice, but I couldn't help it. "Right?"

"I'm sorry, Yared, but there were . . . complications. The pirates have made things too dangerous at the moment." Mom looked at Dad, who nodded.

"That's right. You'll still give your speech. It will just be delivered remotely from your cousin's residence on Old Earth, while your mother and I handle the Werari Referendum and the ongoing search for Adwa on the *Benevolence*."

I couldn't believe it. This was horrible! Not only would I miss the Royal Trials, not only would I lose the only opportunity to pilot an exo I'd probably ever get, but I STILL had to give my speech? It was like the universe tripped me, laughed, and then kicked me when I was down. I was doomed. Forever doomed.

"It's settled!" Balamba Ras roared, and pounded the table at the same time. "Now then, on to serious matters. Trade in-system has . . ."

Everyone turned back to the briefing table, while I felt my spirits crumble into glittering space dust. Even Besa leaning against me couldn't cheer me up. No Royal Trials. No exploring a new space station and making friends. No piloting an exo, now or in the foreseeable future. Just—I swallowed an urge to groan—*reflection.*

How could this trip get any worse?

CHAPTER FIVE

Three hours after my fate was determined, I watched a group of warships as they performed maneuvers before they approached the space station. There were five in total: four hornet-shaped scouts and a larger battleship with flared wings that reminded me of a hawk.

"Hybrid fighters," Uncle Moti said, pointing toward the smaller four.

We stood on one of the docking pads on the uppermost Axum ring, waving goodbye to my parents as they headed to the *Benevolence* to meet with the IU. We were still waiting on our transport, and as I watched the warships approach, I grew more and more impressed with the moves they executed. Barrel rolls, loops, even some synchronized turns. That had to be our ride! They were showing out to impress, and their sleek design and shiny exterior screamed royal transport. I wondered if they would let me do a barrel roll or two.

"Why are they called hybrids?" I asked. "What does that mean?"

Uncle Moti gestured at the ships as they spread into an escort formation around us. "It means they're just as capable operating within the planet's atmosphere, with gravity and other forces to contend with, as they are here in orbit. Very versatile, if a little too dependent on their speed rather than firepower. Unlike that wolf right there." He pointed at the battleship. "That's a light cruiser."

Uncle Moti stroked his beard for a second, then turned to me. "Based on your observation, what's their plan?" he asked.

I blinked. Why would they need a plan to give us a lift? "Um . . . what?"

"Their plan. Their tactics. Why fly out with this ship arrangement?"

I groaned . . . in my head, not out loud. I wasn't that wild. But Uncle Moti loved testing me on strategy and it was so annoying. Yes, it helped me back when the Werari invaded Addis Prime. Did I enjoy it? Definitely not.

I racked my brain for several seconds, then shrugged. "I'm not sure. Maybe it's the standard arrangement for a welcome party?" Uncle Moti frowned at me, and I sighed. "I guess that was too much to ask for."

The third member of our four-unit squad sucked her teeth in annoyance. The Ibis slid her faceshield open, squinted at the ships, then flicked the tinted visor back down over her eyes.

"It's protocol," she said. Besa, the fourth and final member of our little party, rumbled in her chest. I made a face at her. She didn't have to *always* agree with the Ibis.

Uncle Moti raised an eyebrow but only motioned for her to go on.

"Protocol probably says to respond to unknown ships in the system in a certain way. That cruiser likely has enough shields and firepower to do some serious damage against any opponent, and the hybrids would carry information back in-system, outrunning whatever pursuit ships intruders might have. Security and planning."

The Ibis finished her speech, and I rolled my eyes. Show-off. "But we're not an unknown ship. We're their passengers!" Uncle Moti gave me a weird look, as if I'd started speaking gibberish. "Right?"

Uncle Moti shook his head, though I noticed he never took his eyes off the ships as they docked at the station. "No. Why would they give us a ride? No, no, no, my boy—this is our ride here."

He pointed to a greenish-orange rusted transport shuttle

all the way on the next docking pad. Don't let the color fool you, it was even uglier than you think. I mean, it was the *ugliest* ship I'd ever seen. Like a flying pig. No offense to pigs. The weird green color seemed to move on its own if the light hit it just right, like it was covered in slime paint. More of its hull was dented than in good repair. A cheery-looking woman emerged from the pig ship onto the docking pad. I guessed she was the captain, as she waved her hands to get our attention. I sighed. The universe loved to kick me when I was down.

"And by the way," Uncle Moti continued, "you were nearly one hundred percent correct about the ships, young lady. You just missed two things."

"What?" the Ibis asked.

"Those ships are in a patrol formation. Most likely—though I can't be sure—they're sweeping the system for pirates."

Right. The pirates Balamba Ras had mentioned. He'd seemed so intent on discussing how to handle them now that the Axum space station was in the system. He had spent the rest of the meeting trying to wrestle commitments out of my parents to spare no expense in hunting down the villains. Apparently, the leader was a crafty pilot who could strike and disappear into the space junk orbiting Old Earth like a shadow.

Uncle Moti was still speaking. "Secondly, the light cruiser would triumph over *most* opponents. Not all of them. Axum would show them a thing or two."

"That seems . . . confident, at least for you," I said. "How can you be so sure?"

He turned back to the screen and stared at the cruiser. Something like regret, or maybe longing, crossed his face. Then he pivoted and began to walk toward our transport. "Because Axum designed those ships."

So, let's sum up the bad news. Instead of heading for the Royal Trials, the greatest video game tournament happening this side of the galaxy, I was bundled into a tiny oinking shuttle and sent to my cousin's beat-up spaceport on Old Earth, nearly six hours away.

(Uncle Moti was worried about being too flashy if there really were pirates around.)

Instead of meeting new friends and maybe becoming, oh, I don't know, popular, only a select group of people knew where I was going.

(Uncle Moti was worried about someone trying to take advantage of me.)

And instead of boldly stepping into my new life as a prince, I was skulking away from a problem that may or may not even really exist!

(Uncle Moti was . . . you know what, it would probably be best just to assume Uncle Moti was paranoid.)

The man himself was in the cockpit in front of us, humming and singing snatches of an old song. I'd heard him sing it before back in Addis Prime, but only when he thought I wasn't listening, or when he was concentrating on something with 100 percent of his attention.

"Summer skies," he sang, "soaring on freedom's wings. Hmm-hm-hmmmm . . ." His voice trailed off as he hopped on the comm to talk to someone, and I smiled. Some things would never change, even amid everything else that had for us, and that felt good.

Anyway, there was some good news buried in all this mess. Two tiny little bright sides. You probably heard me mention them earlier, not that they were super enthused to be tagging along. Still, I knew they'd come around eventually.

"I hate you," the Ibis said.

"Don't say that," I muttered, trying for the fiftieth time to get the old harness restraints in the rusty pig shuttle to stop trying to strangle me. Apparently, the automated restraints had only two settings—*limp noodle* or *I hate that you can breathe.*

"Mrowr."

I rolled my eyes. "Of course you're taking her side. But you would've missed me."

Besa, crammed into a tiny space behind us that I guessed was a cargo hold, pressed her ears flat to her skull and hissed something absolutely inappropriate.

"Seriously," the Ibis continued, "the only reason my parents let me come to Harar Station was because they thought I'd be getting a Meshenitai's astrogator training. Having someone trained on advanced navigation programming would be useful back on the farms. Not to play rent-a-friend for bored royalty."

I winced. "Jeez, I'm sorry I invited you. You could've said no."

"It wasn't an invitation. That's not what your silly station AI said. 'Lij Yared formally requests your presence on a perilous journey across the system.'"

"I asked Azaj to see if you wanted to come," I protested, slowly losing oxygen to the harness's grip. "Not make you."

Besa flicked my shoulder with her tail. "Mrowr."

"What does that even mean?"

"It means," the Ibis said, leaning over and yanking on a strap I couldn't reach, freeing up my chest and lungs to work normally, "people—and AIs apparently—are going to take your words very seriously every time you speak. My *prince*. People with privilege, like you, should wield it carefully, like you would a weapon, because you might end up hurting someone without realizing. So maybe, just maybe, you should think about what you're asking before you open your mouth."

The Ibis folded her arms and stared at the screen on the dented wall in front of us. It separated the passenger section from the flight deck. Some newsvid played about protests on Old Earth, involving construction for the Royal Trials. I ignored it. Missing out still stung.

"Okay, I'm sorry. You're right—like always. I will try to watch what I'm saying and asking."

"Good." She made a noise of disgust at the protests and gestured for the screen to turn off. "Where are we going anyway? Your uncle was real tight-lipped about it."

I shrugged. "The remains of some old fortress that used to guard Axum's brain while the space station was being built. Best vacation ever."

Silence filled the shuttle. When I glanced over, the Ibis's jaw was practically in her lap.

"What?" I asked.

"The *Amba*? We're going to the *Amba*?"

"Sort of. The remains, but yeah. Apparently it was destroyed, but my cousin said he gathered what they could find and built a small spaceport on Old Earth. You've heard of it?"

"Heard of it?" The Ibis was practically vibrating in her seat, that's how excited she was. "It had the *only* library for historical astrogation technology! I wonder if that managed to survive when the station was converted into New Amba. I was watching some docuvids on its design, and apparently they had databases there with the most recordings on inter-galactic astrogation theory and how theoretical flight paths can be extrapolated from the inference of light protons traveling . . ." Her voice faded as both Besa and I almost passed out, trying to decipher what she was saying.

"Sorry," she said.

"Sooo," I said, a smile growing on my face. "I did a good thing inviting you along."

She shot me a look, then reached over and flicked the strap she'd just fixed on my harness. The restraints glee-fully tried to turn my ribs into shiro.

"Point taken," I wheezed.

Just then, the overhead speaker hissed and an automated voice blared out, informing us that we were beginning our final approach to the *Amba*'s spaceport. The place appeared on the screen in front of us, and I sighed. It didn't look like much. A star-shaped building with a tram system and a few satellite dishes. So this was where I'd be spending my time, while the greatest game to be played unfolded on the same planet. How the mighty had fallen.

"On the bright side," I said to Besa while the Ibis strained at her harness to get a better look at our destination, "at least one of us is happy to be here. Looks like it's just you and me on the pity rocket, Besa. We'll get through this together. Right?"

"MROWR!"

Besa wasn't even listening to me. Her tail flicked left and right impatiently as she stared out the window. Several giant quad-lifts floated in the docking bay we were heading to, the automated cargo transports following guidance lasers to their assigned berths. Besa stared at the lasers, and I could practically hear the plans she made to chase them.

I sighed. "Never mind. Just one ticket for the pity rocket, please, destination Sad Town, population me."

The Ibis stopped cackling gleefully and made an empathetic noise. "Sorry, I forgot you had your speech coming up."

Right. The speech. I'd actually managed to forget about that, too . . . until now.

I felt each and every second pass in slow motion. Excruciatingly slow motion. Who knew that when you had the speech of a lifetime coming up, time slowed for some reason? Each tiny nanosecond felt like an entire day. Uncle Moti made me rehearse it as we made our final approach, and nobody laughed or yawned, so I figured it wasn't too bad. Still, I was so nervous! I guess it was like taking a test, or maybe even performing in a virtual masinko recital.

Everything is stressful until the moment you have to start, and then it's over in the blink of an eye.

At least I hoped so.

The Ibis glanced over at me, as if reading my thoughts. She smiled apologetically and returned to checking out the transport for dangers as we neared our docking pad. Part of her training, I guess. Not that there were many threats around, unless someone could die of a boredom attack. There was only one screen on the shuttle. It reminded me of the oval-shaped buses we rode in and out of the kebeles back home. And once I started thinking about home, I couldn't stop. What were the other students at Addis Prime Primary doing? Mrs. Marjani, my favorite teacher, had sent me a data package for my wrist comm loaded down with . . . ugh . . . with homework. She'd even recorded surprise lectures that only played if I tried to skip ahead in the lessons.

Who does that? Teachers, I swear.

And the HKO . . . would it ever be the same without its greatest champion? I sniffled. Now who would absolutely destroy the competition and remind them of the futility of their efforts? Think of the gamers!

An alert materialized in the middle of the transport. "What's that?" I asked.

Uncle Moti, who for some unknown reason could nap on command, popped awake. He looked around, then nodded toward the screen, which winked on again. It showed a magnified view of my parents' approach to the IU. "Looks like the Emperor and Empress made it."

The courier ship carrying my parents drew closer to the *Benevolence*, the IU space station, and all the other vessels nearby had to retreat a safe distance. I tried to count them—every ship, every satellite, every comm array in orbit—but there were so many! I thought Addis Prime had a busy rush hour in the morning, but the traffic around the *Benevolence* made it seem like a stroll through the market. Giant gas haulers, ore miners, luxury yachts, and hundreds of transports like the one we were on crowded together in queues, all trying to dock. I bet the line for the bathrooms was ridiculous.

But it was the planet around which the *Benevolence* orbited that grabbed and held my attention. Blue and green and white, it shone in the blackness of space like my mother's imperial jewels. Water covered most of its surface, and clouds covered the rest.

"Old Earth," I said.

We all drank in the beauty of the planet where humans first took to the stars. Where Axum first rose to prominence and ushered in a period of incredible advancement. It was like . . . I could feel my ancestors there with me in that moment. Guiding me. Helping me.

Now if only they could give my speech for me.

"Hey, what's that?" The Ibis pointed toward the left side of the screen, where another squad of warships zoomed by in formation. They looked like the battle cruiser that had come to meet us, along with a few larger crafts. They all had weapons that pointed ominously outward. The ships also had the same emblem shining on their hulls as the *Benevolence* had on its spinning torus.

"They're IU ships," I said. "What are they—"

Uncle Moti pointed to a solitary ship towing something down to the planet. I'd missed it in all the traffic.

"Looks like the pirates struck again," he said quietly.

I squinted, then stepped to the screen and fiddled with the controls. It was a basic model, but some features were universal. Seconds later, I had the view centered on the IU ships, zoomed all the way in. "It's a comm array," I said. "A big one. But why would they attack that? There's nothing valuable on board."

"It's not what's on it," the Ibis said quietly. "It's what it provides."

I gawked at her. "What?"

But she didn't answer. Instead, she glanced at Uncle Moti, then pursed her lips and folded her arms. I looked between the two of them. There was something they weren't telling me. I glared at my uncle, and he sighed.

"I'll tell you later" was all he said. "For now, focus on your speech. This is important, Yared."

I grunted. "I still don't get why I have to make the speech," I said, fidgeting with my Radial.

Uncle Moti frowned, but not in disappointment. (I think . . . but honestly, I wouldn't be surprised.) It was in the way adults do when they're figuring out whether to treat you as the child they remember or the adult you're becoming.

"It's because," he finally said, "you are a prince of Axum. *The* prince. Do you know what that means? You are the heir apparent to an empire that, decades ago, was a protector and symbol of peace. Of power. But Axum fell out of the galaxy and everyone's minds after the Werari attacked, and while some people will be happy that we have returned, not everyone will be. When a great tree falls, new trees climb to the light."

He dropped to one knee and grabbed my shoulders with his hands. "By standing in front of the Intergalactic Union, many of whom have planets and systems who've benefited from Axum technology, you not only announce to the galaxy that Axum has truly returned, you make it clear that we will be here for generations to come. You are the message bearer and the message. That is why your speech is important."

"Speech, speech, speech," I grumbled. "I'm never talking to anyone ever again after this."

"Oh no," the Ibis said in a dry, mocking tone. "Whatever will we do?"

Uncle Moti laughed, and I made a face at the Ibis just as our transport docked with New Amba. We'd arrived, and I took a deep breath to steady my nerves.

"Relax," my uncle said. "We'll have a few hours to unwind. I can show you around, though my memory of the place is vague. Only got to tour it virtually before communication was lost. I do remember a good tej lounge somewhere on the upper decks." He rubbed his beard thoughtfully, and I snickered. If there was tej nearby, Uncle Moti would sniff it out.

Maybe it wouldn't be so bad. A few hours from now and it'd be all over and I could enjoy sightseeing around the space station. Maybe even get a chance to go down to Earth and check out the Royal Trials. I was working out the best way to convince Uncle Moti that the game arenas would have tej when the transport's hatch hissed open. I turned to the exit, only to freeze.

Six exo troopers with bright red power armor stood in the corridor outside the access tube connecting us to the space station. Their faces were helmeted so we couldn't make them out, and they cradled dual stun batons in their arms.

I stared at them.

They didn't move.

"Hi!" I said. "Yared, party of four?"

The Ibis groaned, and Besa swished her tail in annoyance. But before anyone could respond, a familiar face appeared. Well, a masked face. It was Mesfina. He wore a long, floor-length robe dyed a vivid scarlet color, with flared sleeves that hid his hands, while his customary black-and-silver uniform looked impeccable, as usual.

"Apologies, everyone, apologies," Mesfina said, waving at me in such a goofy way that I couldn't help but wave back. "There's been . . . an incident, so Balamba Ras asked me to personally escort you."

Uncle Moti stepped forward. "Incident? What incident? And we were led to believe the council hearing would not occur for a few hours yet."

Mesfina raised both arms in an *I'm just the messenger* gesture. "Some sort of pirate attack. But I can assure you that everything is under control. The guards here"—he gestured to the armored troops—"will accompany Yared to the staging room and make sure no unauthorized personnel get inside. General Berihun, the Negus and Negiste asked for you to coordinate with them to handle Axum's response. So, if you'll follow me . . ." He gestured ahead of him. I glanced up at Uncle Moti, who hadn't moved.

"If there is a security concern," my uncle continued, "Yared stays with me. No one who hasn't been vetted by me personally guards the prince. No one."

Mesfina flipped his cloak behind him so that he could fold his arms across his chest. I could tell he was irritated at Uncle Moti's objections. "General Berihun, I understand your reluctance. But this isn't Axum territory, unfortunately, and the IU has strict rules regarding visitors. Believe me, I know how strict they are. If I could change them, I would. But if you want to speak to Balamba Ras, you can. He's talking with the Emperor and Empress right now. Yared will just have to miss his speech."

I finally picked up on the difficult situation we were in. If the council was convening now, I had to give my speech. Uncle Moti had just finished stressing the importance of it, of me, to Axum and its future. But pirates had attacked that comm array, and by the looks of things, they hadn't been caught. That meant we had to follow IU protocols, no matter how uncomfortable that made Uncle Moti, who always made sure he did what he thought was best for my safety. Even if it meant being bundled up like I was a fragile child.

That was it. I was tired of the paranoia. First the pig shuttle, now this? I couldn't take it.

Uncle Moti and Mesfina were still arguing in that way

that adults argue where they don't raise their voices or scowl or stomp around, but instead they smile while saying things that sound one way but actually mean something totally different. At least I think Mesfina was smiling, as it was hard to tell with the mask. His eyes crinkled, but maybe he had gas, I don't know. It was confusing, but I guess growing up did that to you. The Ibis and I exchanged a glance, like two kids whose parents bumped into each other at the market and now wouldn't leave. I had to do something.

"Why don't I go with the Ibis and Besa to give my speech?" I said loudly, stepping into their conversation. "It has to be safer than staying here, right? They can keep an eye on me while you talk with Mom and Dad. That way I can give the best speech anyone has ever heard and still be protected." I glanced at the Ibis. "Right?"

"Right." The Ibis nodded. She pulled up a schematic of New Amba on her wrist comm and expanded it in the air between us. She zoomed in on a subsection and placed three glowing pins in different locations. "According to the schematics I downloaded earlier, there are three safe rooms reserved for visiting diplomats—which Yared *technically* is. Besa and I can secure him in one of those after his speech and wait for the next move. Right, Besa?"

My lioness Guardian shook herself. "Mrowr."

I raised an eyebrow at that. "You will not sit on me."

Uncle Moti still seemed hesitant. "Well," he said, then fell silent.

"I have to give the speech, right?"

He rubbed his chin again and sighed. "The one time you decide to act like a prince is the one time I'm afraid to let you do it."

I straightened and gazed off into the distance. "We must not let fear—"

Besa's nudge against the back of my knees knocked me off balance into a very unprincely tumble. I squawked in outrage, and the Ibis smothered a laugh. Uncle Moti's eyes twinkled as he helped me up, and Mesfina chuckled, his laugh muffled by the mask. I dusted myself off, solemnly swearing to find a magnet large enough to suspend an annoying metal kitty in midair until I felt like letting her down.

First, however, I had a speech to make. My adoring public awaited.

CHAPTER SIX

Ten minutes after we separated from Uncle Moti, we were already in trouble.

"Well, how was I supposed to know he was real?" I asked Mesfina, who was escorting us through Balamba Ras's headquarters. "I thought he was a holovid!"

"He was preparing a jebena for visitors," the Ibis said with an impatient sigh. Apparently, *my* unjust treatment by the fortress's personnel was clashing with her desire to learn everything in the galaxy. "Didn't you smell the coffee roasting behind him?"

"Why didn't he just get a bunamech to do it? Then I wouldn't have been confused."

"Because, my prince," Mesfina answered, "not everyone is fortunate enough to own a bunamech."

Mesfina stopped at a junction just ahead of us, hands clasped behind his back, his black-and-silver mask gleaming in the bright lights of the docking bay.

"Look around. We aren't what we used to be. In the years

since Axum fell out of history, so did the galaxy's interest in exploring. Without our technology—and the people who knew how to use it—Old Earth and the rest of the colonies in the Sol-Luna System forgot about us. They made do with the few shipping routes safe enough to travel and taxed the vessels willing to travel them heavily. Now the IU is content to remain where they are, while the rest of the system grows crowded and the people become desperate. And we can't do anything about it, stuck here in the dying memory of a destroyed fortress."

A note of bitterness had entered Mesfina's voice. He must've realized it because he shook himself and gave a wry chuckle. "But now that you're here, my prince, all that can change."

"It can?" I asked, glancing at the Ibis and Besa, who both shrugged in response. (Have you ever seen a half-ton Guardian lioness shrug? It's like a tank hopping up and down.)

"Absolutely. Adwa is the key. You are the key holder."

Mesfina motioned us to follow him, and after another shared glance, we did. He led us through the junction, down a small corridor, and into a transportation hub where a cluster of hovertrams floated under a holomap of New Amba. Even though I counted ten magnetic tracks embedded in the floor leading to the docking bay tram stop, most of them were dusty and covered in tarps. Only one even floated, and Mesfina had to bang a gloved fist on the cone-like nose of the tram in order to get the doors to open. We hopped aboard and—after a shuddering jerk—swept out of the docking bay as Mesfina activated a large display that rose out of the tram floor. "This is who we are," he said.

It was a hologram of New Amba. The facility was shaped like a star. The points of the star were connected by a ring that allowed the trams to quickly circle the fortress. The one we were riding was highlighted in silver as it passed through the fortress, but Mesfina pressed a button and the display zoomed out until we could see all of Old Earth and the space around it.

"This is who we could be."

It was . . . amazing. Spectacular.

Now the star fortress hologram floated in space. Ships passed above and beneath it on their way to Old Earth. Several solar farms captured energy from the rays of the sun at the center of the system and stored them in enormous battery collectors, which would be harvested and transported and replaced with empty collectors. But the giant object that Mesfina pointed out dwarfed everything. It looked like a three-dimensional parallelogram.

"That is where Adwa belongs," Mesfina whispered. "If Harar Station, with the thrones of the Negus and Negiste, is the heart of the Axum Empire, then Adwa Station is its mind. Once the two are reunited, we can unlock the star fortress's navigation capabilities once again. We can explore! But only you can make that happen, my prince."

There was pure joy in Mesfina's voice, and I couldn't help but share in it. I grinned, and Besa roared. Even the Ibis clenched her fists in excitement. Everyone wanted to travel the stars again. I wanted to explore and to meet new people and make new friends. The Ibis wanted to learn as much as she could to help her family. Besa wanted . . . well, to be honest I had no idea. I'd have to ask her.

I turned to Mesfina. "If we find Adwa, people back on Addis Prime could come visit, right?"

Mesfina nodded. "Exactly."

Haji's face popped into my mind. I'd be able to see my friends! And the Ibis . . . her parents and sisters could come visit. I took a deep breath. "All right. What do I have to do?"

The tram plunged into darkness as we reentered the next section of New Amba, and the hologram disappeared. We entered a brightly lit station with dozens of small drones buzzing around, performing maintenance, while others hovered around a giant figure who sent them on their way with a flick of his fingers. He scowled as the tram slowed to a stop, and I gulped.

Even without his spider-mech, Balamba Ras still looked fierce.

"He looks like he wants to use you for rocket fuel," the Ibis whispered.

I gulped again.

Mesfina placed a hand on my shoulder for reassurance, drawing me away from the others for a moment of privacy. "You asked what you could do to help? Lend me your Radial."

"The Radial?" I asked, staring at my wrists. Why did he need that?

"Yes! With it, I can bypass the IU checkpoints and finally explore all of Old Earth with a proper search. Adwa is out there, Yared. I can feel it! But the bureaucrats and their red tape are preventing anyone without high-level credentials from even asking questions! They're looking for it themselves, you know."

"They are?"

Mesfina nodded, his modulated voice dropping in volume until it was barely a staticky whisper. "They are. Everyone wants Axum's technology, even if no one wants Axum to return. But I have something they don't—a clue."

He rubbed his hands together thoughtfully. "You're a gamer, Yared. Have you seen the uproar with regard to the Royal Trials?"

I perked up. "Actually, I did see something on a news-vid . . . about protests over where the matches were being held. What does that have to do with Adwa?"

"I can't say too much," he said, glancing around. The Ibis and Besa were preoccupied with the bots outside the tram. "There are eyes and ears everywhere. But we picked up on a secure transmission that talked about strange ruins near one of the proposed match sites. If we can use your Radial to bypass the checkpoints, and then get you into a match, it's possible we can find a clue as to where Adwa is."

Go to the Royal Trials? That was . . . that was almost too good to be true! Even if it was just one of the proposed locations. I opened my mouth to say I would—I *really* thought that's what I was going to say—but instead, what came out was: "Sorry, Mesfina, but . . . I can't. Uncle Moti and my parents think it's too dangerous. I wish I could." I shrugged.

Mesfina straightened. It was hard to tell with his face hidden behind the blank silver mask, but something in his demeanor changed. He seemed to grow . . . colder.

But I had to be imagining it, because a second later, he was clapping me on the shoulder.

"Of course, Lij Yared. We have to listen to the Negus and Negiste. It was just an idea. Oh, it looks like they're waiting for us." Balamba Ras had begun to stomp forward, a trio of drones following him. "I think it is time for your speech."

I ignored the snarling ax head of the Bulgu as it slashed through the air inches away from my head and instead continued my speech.

". . . and that's why I'm here today. As a boy. As a survivor of not one, but two Werari invasions. Their horrific campaigns terrorized, abused, and traumatized thousands of people—adults and children.

"I am here as a citizen of Axum. Not to threaten or bribe, but to warn. I've seen the lies the Werari spin. The monster they unleashed on my home wasn't the Bulgu—that was just its physical appearance. The real monster is their greed.

"And though I'm here as a prince, it's not to claim some sort of superiority or to take back whatever lost power some might think we want. It's to help. To defend against the Werari. To reunite the people scattered around the galaxy by their attack. And to help other nations the way the Axum of years past did: Because a united galaxy is a thriving galaxy. I hope you'll join us. Thank you."

I looked into the floating camera-drone hovering a meter away and watched the red light fade to black. My mouth was incredibly dry, almost like I'd been chewing on a rug for an hour. (Don't ask how I knew what that felt like.) I took a drink from the glass of water on the hovering podium in front of me as the holographic Bulgu, Gebeya, and Harar Station faded away.

Was that it? The speech was over, and I couldn't help but feel . . . like there was something missing. If I had stood in front of the entire IU council, there would've been a buzz of conversation. Discussion about the Werari, talks about Axum's return and the future, and maybe even—dare I dream—a thunderous round of applause. Instead, there was this hollow feeling in the pit of my stomach. One I couldn't fill with sambusas, no matter how hard I tried. And I definitely planned on trying. I sighed and gathered up my notes.

Just then, someone clapped in the back of the room. I squinted against the glare of the podium lights. I stood on an integrated presentation stage, in the center of a small conference room. The clear glass of the platform was embedded with hundreds of rows of alternating projectors and cameras. Workstation chairs surrounded the circular stage, and as I looked around the room, the stern faces of the audience began to fade away. I'd been speaking to a crowd of stenotechs: holograms that recorded what they witnessed before collapsing into data streams that beamed themselves across the planetary system. The data streams were then only accessible by the stenotechs' owners or another person they authorized. The ultimate DM. I knew a couple students back in Addis Prime Primary who would absolutely drool over that.

"Well done," a voice called out.

The podium lights finally turned off, and I saw the speaker, the only audience member who didn't fade away. He was a tall, skinny, older boy, with deep brown skin and clear glasses that rippled with light around the edges. He wore a silver ceremonial tunic a lot like my gold one, the edges trimmed in glimmering black thread, and matching pants. A small silver necklace was his only accessory, with a strange charm that looked halfway melted hanging from it. He sat in one chair and propped his feet up on another.

I hesitated. The Ibis and Besa were a couple rooms over, watching a stream of the speech. Uncle Moti was still with Balamba Ras talking about the pirate attacks. I didn't know if I would've appreciated them here or if being by myself had been better for my nerves. Either way, I was glad it was over.

I probably should've gone to find Besa and the Ibis, but the older boy seemed friendly enough. And it had been so long since I'd had a chance to make a new friend. After a second, I hopped off the stage and sat down nearby.

"Thanks," I said. "Glad I had at least one live person here."

The older boy laughed. "Ahh, these virtual sessions aren't that bad. And besides, when's the last time you got to talk without an adult interrupting you? Me? I'm thinking I could get used to a life of speeches. Especially if it comes with free all-you-can-eat sambusas."

Right on cue, a drone hummed by with a platter of steaming sambusas piled on top.

I leaned forward and pointed. "You, sir, make excellent points."

He shot to his feet and bowed, tucking the necklace in. "Jemal Ammanuel."

"Lij Yared Heywat of Axum," I said, returning the gesture.

Jemal whistled. "A prince? I'm in the presence of royalty. Well, then . . ." He snatched several sambusas from the drone and tossed one to me. "It's common to bring gifts when introduced to royalty, so please accept this humble and yet delightfully flaky offering. It took me hours to prepare."

I snorted, and he grinned. We dropped back into our workstation chairs and got busy with our snacks. The sambusa was incredible. Light and flaky and steaming hot. I could've eaten thirty of them. When I finished, I sighed and reclined. "So where are you from?" I asked.

Jemal flapped a hand. "Here and there. Traveled a lot."

"Me too. Around the galaxy?"

He laughed. "I wish. No, I mean around here." He pointed to the floating display of Earth, its moon, and the IU.

"You're from here? Old Earth?" I said, staring in disbelief.

"Yep. Born and raised. My mother was the leader of one of the largest terrestrial factions, and my father used to be a pilot. So I bounced around between the IU space station and Old Earth a lot, which sucks. Just when I'm getting comfortable in one spot I have to leave, you know?"

The thing is, I did know. Before I knew anything about Axum beyond Uncle Moti's stories, we'd traveled a lot, too. Moving from city to city, from school to school, never staying long enough to make real friends. I mean, I knew now that it was for my own protection, but it still sucked.

Another drone flew by, this time with a platter of juice bulbs. I grabbed two and tossed one to Jemal. "So what're you doing in here? Something for your dad?"

He looked off into the distance for a bit. "Yeah, right," he muttered sarcastically. "No, I'm here because this is apparently one of the safest rooms on the whole space station. Mom made me come when the station went on lockdown. Again."

"Something like this has happened before?"

He shrugged. "It happens a few times a *month*. Pirates

are always causing problems in space, and all the traffic coming in and out of the system and up and down from Earth doesn't help, either. A few weeks ago, a cargo transport accidentally clipped a comms array and knocked out communication to a third of the planet. Mom was heated. She said if she ever found out who did it, she would cancel all their delivery contracts to the planet. And since our faction is the largest, that's a pretty big threat. My guess is that's what happened again. Those comm arrays are on a preset orbital pattern, but cargo pilots don't care. They'll try to shave a light-minute off their time and take any shortcut they can. Some poor nebula-head probably obliterated another satellite, and now we all have to suffer. At least the juice is good.

"Anyway," he continued after practically eating the juice bulb, "it's not all bad. I found out if you connect to the network in the conference room, you can stream almost anything. And no interruptions means I can watch the opening ceremony of the Royal Trials."

My jaw dropped. "You're watching the Royal Trials?"

Jemal tapped his glasses and grinned. So *that's* why the edges were rippling with light. They were augmented reality glasses, like what I used to play the HKO back on Addis Prime! Maybe if I could get logged in, I could still at least watch some of the opening matches. It wasn't anything close to participating, but still . . . it was worth a shot, right?

"Do you have another pair of glasses I can borrow?" I asked hopefully.

He shook his head, and my spirits dropped. "Sorry, Yared. Just got the one, and it took me forever to save up for them."

I sighed and sat back down at my workstation. So much for that idea.

"Buuuut," he continued, pursing his lips and drumming his fingers on the workstation, "I *have* hooked them up to the stage before. It takes more power, and we'll have to disconnect the camera feed to plug the glasses into it, but then we can both watch."

I shot up. "Yes!"

"Are you sure? Don't you have to ask your people?"

I shook my head. "Nope, as long as I stay in here, we should be good."

Jemal grinned. "All right! Here, plug the glasses into the back of the camera. I'll queue up the stage's software."

I was practically bouncing as I disconnected the wire from the security camera and plugged it into the glasses. The frames flashed twice, and then Jemal threw up his hands. "Teff of the saints. I can't get around the security lock. We're stuck."

I groaned. So close! All I wanted was just to get a glimpse of the Royal Trials. Not even the whole thing! Just a piece, a taste, a sliver of a slice. But—

Wait. I thought about if for a second. "We just need to get around security?" I asked.

He nodded.

I took a deep breath and then flicked open my Radial. Jemal gasped, but I was already moving toward his workstation and sitting down. He hastily retreated. "System," I said, "bypass meeting room communication security."

The Radial spun around my wrists and then said, "Confirm temporary security clearance?"

"Confirm."

Jemal scrambled to another workstation, then threw a thumbs-up into the air. "Got it!" he said. "Got the feed. Come on, it's starting."

We grabbed seats nearest to the stage, and I let out a whoop of joy as the lights dimmed. Suddenly, exos materialized onstage amid fireworks. The speakers throughout the room rang with cheers from virtual fans. Jemal and I cheered along with them as a hologram avatar of an older teen boy wearing a custom flight suit appeared in front of us. Images rippled along his arms and legs as he spun in a circle and pumped his fists.

"What's up, Earth?!" he screamed. The cheering doubled

as he raised both arms and twirled around the room. "It's your boy, nanoL0gic, here to welcome you all to the game of games, the wildest competition in the whole galaxy, the one, the only, Royal Triiiiiaaaaaals!"

Three exos dropped from the virtual sky behind him. I gasped. It was the Amir-Nur Clan, the number-one-ranked team from last season. Their armored suits had been fashioned in the style of giant hyenas, with fangs protruding from their helmets and claws painted onto their power boots. Their exos were huge, hulking things that were super powerful and top of the line.

Jemal whistled. "I hear those Hyena-2 units are awesome to pilot. Man, would I love to take a ride in one of those."

I nodded as nanoL0gic grinned and continued speaking. "New season, new game mode! The Nexus has been buzzing about the new format for this year's competition, and your boy is here to tell you that it's all true. Trios will be making its debut, so grab two friends for your squad and get ready. Because this year there's no talisman, no virtual items, no way. One hundred and twenty-eight teams will enter, but only one can be crowned champion. Have you got your spot locked in? Then get ready to battle bots, drones, and—most importantly—each other! Duke it out in your exos for glory and fame."

My heart pounded in anticipation. More and more exos

appeared onstage, followed by giant floating bots. Some of the bots actually looked like giant scrappers. I grinned. I could practically hear the Ibis yelling about the nests they created. More dropped from the ceiling, climbed out of the stage floor, and even cut through the walls in the back of the conference room.

Wait . . . cut through the walls? How was that even—

NanoL0gic raised his hand and pointed out at us. "Remember, gang, keep your head on a swivel and watch each other's backs . . . you never know who might be gunning for you. I'll see you at the after-party! NanoL0gic . . . out."

The teen disappeared, along with the rest of the virtual stadium, leaving me and Jemal . . . and the three menacing scrappers who'd just floated from the smoking hole in the wall.

CHAPTER SEVEN

We stared at the scrappers.

They stared back. The three floated at least eight feet off the floor, their armor streaked in neon orange. Four spindly legs folded beneath them, with stalk-like eyes and multiple thrusters all over their insectoid bodies, making them incredibly maneuverable.

I lifted my finger and pointed at the orange streaks. "Nice decals." Their armored plates were like mirrors; I could see Jemal standing in bewilderment behind his seat next to me.

The three scrappers hovered forward. Their legs unfolded in a manner that suggested they were not for hugging.

"Now hold on," I said. "I'd love to hang out, but I have prior engagements. Like . . . I don't know, getting my teeth pulled. Go polish your heads somewhere."

"Yared," Jemal whispered. "What are you doing?"

I turned to him. "Don't let these bots get you riled up. We see them all the time on Harar Station." Which was true. But there was something different about these scrappers.

For one, they looked larger than the normal bots I'd seen, and they also weren't usually this aggressive. It was almost like they'd been reprogrammed. Still, if they wanted a fight, I was going to give them one.

I grabbed my drink bulb and hurled it at the lead scrapper. The juice splattered across its armor and legs. I ducked down behind a floating chair and peeked around its side, waiting for the sparks to fly. "Take that!" I said.

No sparks appeared.

"*That* was your plan?" Jemal asked. "A juice bulb?"

"I thought it'd short out their circuitry or something."

"You just made them angrier!"

I threw up my hands. "I saw it in a holovid, so I thought it would work!"

The carapace armor of each scrapper slid open just beneath their heads at the same time. Out popped meter-long rods with electric blue tips. Stasis stingers. Great. They floated closer as the stingers cracked and popped menacingly. One spark leapt from a wand to the conference table, shorting out the display and causing it to glitch with a massive *POP*.

I swallowed. "Hey, now, don't take it so personal. I'm sure it'll buff right out. Let me just get someone to help with that . . ."

I tapped my comm link, hoping to alert the Ibis or Besa

or, I don't know, even a custodian bot. Someone. Anyone!

But just as the Ibis popped onto the display above my wrist, the shiny bot lunged forward. The tip of its stasis wand grazed the comm link, and the Ibis fizzled out of view. I yelped as a stinging sensation traveled up my wrist to my elbow.

"Hey!" I shouted. "That stung!"

"Maybe we should—" Jemal started to say, but I grabbed two more juice bulbs from the floating refreshment tray and hurled them at the bots . . . and the stasis wands.

This time, the bulbs exploded in a shower of delightful fruit droplets and hissing electricity. The stasis wand shorted out with a bright flash. I was moving before my eyes had even recovered. I grabbed Jemal's wrist with my left hand. With my right, I flicked my birhani out and snapped it open to its widest length. Sliding it on the floor in front of me, I hopped on and pulled Jemal up with me.

"Hold on!" I shouted, then kicked off the floor. The anti-grav system whirred on, and we were off—grinding across the table, over the stunned and flailing shiny scrappers, and out the hole in the wall. I had no idea what was happening, but between the pirate threat and the three giant robo-bugs trying to make Yared-kebab, the best place for me to be was safely back with Uncle Moti, the Ibis, and Besa.

Now I just had to find them.

*   *   *

New Amba was pure chaos. The corridors were stuffed with people in all the different stages of panic. Some were yelling at one another, while others stared in blank, wide-eyed shock at the few screens that were apparently working. On them, a gaping hole stretched across a large section of the facility, smoke billowing out into the sky.

"Where are we going?" Jemal shouted. He held on to a fistful of my ceremonial robes, which I'd managed to keep clean, thank you very much, even with someone flinging juice bulbs around all willy-nilly.

"I don't know!" I called back over my shoulder. "Anywhere but here."

"They blew it up," a man muttered as he held on to the arm of a small child. "The pirates really blew it up."

I started to pause and let the man know that scrappers were the problem, not pirates, but at that moment, a tug on my sleeve distracted me.

"That's not good," Jemal muttered, pointing at one of the screens. "That looks like the fuel stations."

I saw an opening in the crowd and sped the lightboard through it. "The what?"

"The fuel stations. They pretty much power everything in New Amba. Air recirculation, emergency support, medical bot deployment . . . they all depend on the fuel stations to do their jobs. If they get destroyed, this whole place would be in trouble."

The horror of it all blindsided me. Why would anyone do that? What did they hope to accomplish? When I asked Jemal as much, he shook his head grimly, anger written across his face.

"Some people will do anything to be heard, I guess."

"So are the pirates working with the scrappers? Who even are these people?"

I squeezed the birhani between a tight group of clerks all screaming into comm links just as dead as mine, then stopped in frustration as a cluster of security guards forced their way in the opposite direction. It was absolute pandemonium, and if that wasn't bad enough, the lights began to flicker. I heard a few screams. This was only going to get worse.

Jemal tapped my shoulder and pointed. An access hatch in the wall had just popped open, and out rolled a custodial bot. Of course! The cleaners used a network of access tunnels to travel unimpeded when they made their rounds. I guess ambassadors didn't like to be reminded they made messes, too. At the moment, I was just happy to escape the chaos. I nodded to show I understood, and we slipped inside. I let out a breath of relief. We could make some good time now. The glow of the birhani gave me just enough illumination to see where I was going. I just hoped we were heading in the right direction.

"They call themselves the Fallen," Jemal said suddenly. "The pirates. Apparently, they've been asking for entry into the IU for years and were denied every time. Some silly old rule that no one knew why was on the books but was too much of a hassle to change. I guess the Fallen got fed up begging for attention. Now they're taking drastic action."

"But why sabotage New Amba?" I asked, squinting at directional markings on the tunnel walls. I was starting to regret not paying attention to the briefing the Ibis had given on the shuttle over. "That doesn't make any sense."

"Like I said, they want to be heard. Look, up ahead." He pointed to another hatch, and I crawled closer. "That should be it."

"You know where we are?"

"Yep. C'mon." Before I could ask him just exactly where that was, he hopped off and pulled the hatch open. Blinking red light spilled inside as he exited the maintenance tunnel. I hesitated, then disengaged the birhani and followed him, collapsing the board into my comm link. At least the stasis stinger hadn't disabled that.

We stepped into a wide, empty corridor. It looked like a side passageway that linked the main corridors of New

Amba with the merchant quarters. It was dotted with interactive displays advertising the latest fads: programmable temporary tattoos that changed when you tapped them; floating salon-drones that styled or cut your hair as you walked; even several ads for the Royal Trials, including a full-sized exo demo that encased you in a simulated power armor suit of your choice, like you were right in the match. I admit I looked at that one longer than I probably should have. When Jemal stopped at an intersection to check the virtual map display for the module we were in, I nearly ran him over.

"What's wrong?" I asked.

He shook his head. "Nothing. Come on—let's go this way."

I squinted at my personal map on my Radial. The shimmering icon representing me (a magnificent and deadly lion roaring, of course) said we were moving farther away from the shuttle docks, not closer. I groaned.

"We're going the wrong way." I tapped the shuttle hangar icon and read out the route. Half the directions were blinking red. "Look, we need to head back toward the restaurant module and then take the tram to the docking bay. Do you think the tram is working?"

"Yared," Jemal whispered.

"Maybe the fuel stations didn't fail completely. Hopefully

it still has power, because I'm definitely not trying to climb seven flights of station ladder-stairs while wearing this ceremonial outfit. Do you know how much I sweat? I'm going to look like a wet rag by the time I get on the shuttle."

"Yared!"

I wiped my hands on my tunic. Were they already sweating just thinking about the journey? My pores betrayed me. Old soggy-palmed Yared. I'd never be able to get rid of that nickname. "Listen, do you have a spare napkin or something? My hands are just—"

Jemal grabbed me and pulled me out of the intersection. "Shh," he hissed.

"What?"

The older boy shook his head. I strained to hear what had spooked him. At first, I could only make out the gentle hum of the interactive ads behind us. (The exo demo continued to call out to me by name, which only goes to show that you should never click on strange ads.) But then, faintly . . .

"MRAWR."

I knew that roar. I'd been unfairly and inappropriately grounded by that roar not that long ago. It was Besa, and it sounded like she was in trouble.

"Yared, wait!" Jemal rasped. Too late. I was already sprinting down the corridor. Besa's roars echoed again and again, filling the empty darkness until it was almost hard to tell whether she was in front of me or behind. New Amba's emergency systems continued to flash soft red lights that barely illuminated the corridor, but the ringing alarms and the automated voice had stopped. I didn't know if that meant the situation was being resolved, but the space station was still in a near-total lockdown. If it wasn't for all the ads (how did *they* get hooked up with emergency power???) I would've tripped and fallen a dozen times. Instead, I skidded to a stop in one of New Amba's many dining areas.

"Besa!" I shouted.

Everything was in shambles. The two-story eating space, with its walls decorated with art from different IU nations, was normally filled with station personnel eating and laughing in between their shifts, or embassy staff from nationalities from across the galaxy chatting in their traditional uniforms. Usually, floating buffet tables made gentle circuits around the room, and juice bulb drones dispensed refreshments like tej and birz (a honey-water drink Uncle Moti allowed me to have while he sipped his tej). Server-bots would whip away empty plates and replace them with new ones, piled high with wat and tibs and everything in between. But now . . . scrappers buzzed around the room.

I leapt over a pile of destroyed drones, grabbing the juice

bulbs scattered around them, and skidded on a spilled bowl of shiro. Then I ran to the center of the room, where Besa battled more of those scrapper bots. My bionic lioness jumped high, claws swatting left and right as she whipped herself around in midair. Two scrappers went crashing down in a smoking pile of thrusters.

"Besa!"

Her ears cocked toward me, but she didn't take her eyes off the remaining attackers. I started to move toward her, but a scrapper zoomed down out of nowhere, stasis stinger arced and ready to attack. I yelped in surprise and dove out of the way.

"Yared!" someone shouted above me. The Ibis was in the middle of sprinting across a line of food-splattered buffet tables that were hovering a dozen meters in the air. Three scrappers chased her. Her spinning seif cut two of them down, before the third forced her to retreat. "You're supposed to be in the safe room!"

"Yeah, well, the safe room wasn't so safe! Scrappers got in there, too."

"What? How?"

I pointed at the final drone trying to knock her unconscious. "I'd tell you, but it looks like your friend is trying to knock you unconscious. You know, I thought you two were supposed to protect me. I'm filing a complaint. Who's your manager?"

"MROWR!"

I ducked at Besa's warning. A disabled scrapper careened overhead to crash into the wall. "Watch it!" I said.

"Get. To. The. Safe room!" the Ibis yelled.

"There *is* no safe room. It's the total opposite! The unsafe room. It's hazardous. The hazardous room, complete with scrappers and a GIANT HOLE IN THE WALL!" I shouted all of this while dodging bits and pieces of more scrappers, which Besa was disassembling like she was selling them for parts. "Where's Uncle Moti?"

"I don't know! Something's jamming all the emergency systems."

That's why we couldn't get through to anyone. I muttered something rude under my breath and scanned the room, looking for anything that would give us a leg up on the bots.

The Ibis leapt over a bowl piled high with sugar-dusted fruit slices. Her seif lanced out and cut the thrusters from the last scrapper pursuing her, sending it twirling to the ground. The room was blessedly silent for once, though I could hear more buzzing coming from one of the main corridors connecting to the dining room, and the way it grew louder let me know that they would be here soon. The Ibis flipped off the floating table she was on, landing next to me in a crouch.

"Show-off," I said, racking my brain to think of a strategy. Maybe we could hold them off and wait for backup? Maybe Uncle Moti would be here soon. Or the guards. Or . . .

Buzzing echoed down the tunnel on my left. I shook my head. It was no good. More scrappers were already coming, and if we stayed, we'd get flanked. Our best bet was to just run for it and hope the slower drones would be left behind.

When I said as much to the Ibis, she nodded. "I think you're right. The docks are a few modules that way." She pointed toward a hatch at the far side of the room. "Besa!" she called out. "We're heading to the docks. Rearguard pattern four."

Besa roared and bounded over, shaking her spikes free of scrapper parts. I frowned. "Wait, you two have your own attack patterns now? Without telling me? That's rude."

"Oh, for the love of the stars," the Ibis said, rolling her eyes. "Will you take this seriously? More of those drones could be here at any second. We need to get you back to General Moti and regroup."

"I *am* taking it seriously! I just . . . you're creating strategies and tactics with my lioness behind my back. Don't you think that's kind of rude? I thought Besa and I were exclusive, and now I found out she's in an open defensive relationship with you. Explain yourself, cat."

"Mrowr."

"Don't take that tone with me. We're gonna talk about this when we're back on the shuttle transport."

"Mrowr mrowr."

As I gasped at the total *rudeness* of Besa's statement, Jemal's voice came through my wrist comm. He sounded panicked.

"Yared, I found a few of the embassy kids hiding in a storage room, but more of those drones just went by."

The Ibis frowned. "Whoever that is, how is he getting through? Are the emergency systems back online?"

"No," I said, showing her the conference room comm links. "We've got to help those kids. No one knows they're down there. If we leave them behind, there's no telling when they'll be rescued."

"Yared, can you hear me?" Someone screamed in the background, and Jemal shushed them. "It's okay; help is coming. Yared, are you there?"

The Ibis looked uncertain. "We're supposed to get *you* back to the docks. That's our focus."

"So do we just leave them?!"

"No! No, of course not." She bit her lip, then nodded at Besa. "We'll—"

She never got to finish her sentence. The skylight display shattered, revealing the maintenance ducts above it, and the hundreds upon hundreds of scrapper-drones that poured out. They must've been gathering there as we spoke. The air was filled with buzzing, shouts, and the electric zaps of the drones' stasis stingers.

I couldn't hear the Ibis or Besa. I couldn't hear myself shout. I couldn't see anything. Was that a glimpse of Besa's silver armor or a flash of the Ibis's silver-and-black uniform lost among the rusted orange storm of scrappers?

I let out a cry as three of them knocked me to the floor. Sharp pain bloomed in my side. A stasis stinger! I could feel pain spreading before the sensation disappeared altogether. My vision blurred. "Help," I called weakly. "Besa. Ibis. System . . . get . . . help."

The last thing I remembered—before the wave of scrappers overwhelmed my vision—was my Radial flickering. Words flashed and a voice said something, but I couldn't make it out. Just before my eyes closed, just before two more stasis stingers jabbed my side, a shadow descended onto the scrappers on top of me. The buzzing faded.

And then the world drifted away.

CHAPTER EIGHT

There's an argument I can remember having with Uncle Moti. We were packing up to move for the third time a few years back, on our way to the warehouse that would end up being our final home on Addis Prime. This time, the reason behind the sudden escape was because I'd invited a friend over without asking Uncle Moti first. He was beyond upset.

For that matter, so was I.

"You act like I can't have any friends at all!" I'd shouted at him. We were on opposite sides of an empty kebele bus. At the front, the rusty automated driver-bot chattered about the local grav-ball team and recited preprogrammed exclamations about the weather.

"You can have friends," Uncle Moti snapped back. "If you follow my rules."

"Your rules are keeping me cooped up like I'm a wild animal or something."

He slammed his hand on the seat in front of him. "My rules are keeping you safe!"

"Safe from what? Excitement? A life? I'm missing out on everything, all because you won't let me do anything without hovering and controlling me."

I stomped to the rear of the bus and stood in the middle of the aisle, watching my home for the last few months disappear into the Addis Prime evening. It was so unfair! Just when I thought things were getting as close to normal as they could be for someone like me, Uncle Moti had to put me right back in emotionally unfamiliar territory. How was I ever going to have my own life if he wouldn't let me live it?

A long sigh filled the bus. Footsteps approached, but I focused on the scrolling landscape.

"I know this type of life is hard. It's . . . not what I would've chosen for you. But it's what we have. And we make these sacrifices to keep you safe. Even if it means we miss a few things."

His hand landed on my shoulder, and he shook me gently.

"In the end, I pray that you understand why it has to be this way."

I can't remember exactly what we did after that. I want to say we arrived at the warehouse, grabbed a bite to eat, and laughed off the earlier argument over some food. Maybe set up our temporary beds and cleaned up a bit.

But I do remember the raw emotion in Uncle Moti's voice

as he talked about sacrifices. At the time, I thought he was upset about having to leave our home in the middle of the night as well. But maybe it wasn't *where* he was leaving, but who—years ago—he'd had to leave.

Everything hurt.

I opened my eyes to see a giant picture of my face floating above me. It was from the last public event I'd attended, before we'd left for the Sol-Luna System—a public function Axum held in every woreda of Addis Prime at the same time. It was a celebration of their return, and a promise.

"A promise that Axum still remembers our mission," Mom had explained to me. "We asked many different nations from many different worlds to join us, to help connect the galaxy. And yet when the Werari invaded, those nations were left on their own. Now we continue that mission, and hopefully the IU can help. So stand up straight and stop slouching. And don't think I didn't see your wrist comm," she said, pointing at the new device. "Don't let me catch you playing with it during the ceremony."

Mothers, am I right?

Now I was lying down, and I had no idea why that picture was there. Had I hit my head? It looked huge, blocking out the rest of my view. It had to be hundreds of meters wide! Was I dreaming? I blinked slowly, squeezing my eyes shut tight before reopening them. Nope, there I was, still smiling, still in my ceremonial uniform. Strange.

"Hey there, Your Awesomeness, you come here often?" I asked.

Wait.

Something wasn't right. My voice. It sounded strange. Like it was muffled. Like I was in a small space with nowhere for my words to go. That was weird. I turned my head—and suddenly everything made sense. The picture moved with me.

I was wearing a helmet.

My picture wasn't floating above me; it was on the helmet's heads-up display, or HUD. But when had I put on my helmet? The last thing I remembered was heading to rescue Jemal from the scrapper bots, when something had . . .

Besa! The Ibis! I jerked upright . . . and immediately regretted it. My head was throbbing. I tried to hold it, only to realize that I was strapped into a harness-like pilot's seat. My hands and feet were engaged with gloves and pedals, and there were toggles and switches everywhere. In fact, the small space was covered with dials and dim screens. I could just make out what I was wearing behind the glowing picture still obscuring most of the display.

It was an exo suit.

"What is going on?" I muttered. "Why am I in power armor? Some sort of emergency protocol? I swear, if this is one of your safety measures, Uncle Moti, I'm going to hack—I mean, *someone* will hack your door controls again so it can only open halfway. You hear me? Besa! Jemal! Anyone out there?"

But my voice only echoed in my ears. I growled something inappropriate and tried to turn off the HUD so I could get a better look at my surroundings. The glare from my face made everything else really dark in comparison.

"Suit, turn off HUD," I commanded.

Nothing happened.

"Suit, enter low-power mode. Disengage heads-up display."

Still nothing.

I frowned. That was weird. Every exo made in the last decade had voice controls, even in Addis Prime. Axum's Meshenitai exos were more advanced, using neural links for many controls, but they were super state-of-the-art.

"Maybe if I . . . ? Oh, come on, my Radial isn't working, either?" I made a face as I flicked my wrists several times and nothing happened. Without voice controls and without my Radial, I couldn't control the exo!

Unless . . . there was an old trick Uncle Moti had shown me once, back when he used to rebuild cargo-loading exos at one of his many extra jobs back on Addis Prime. He called them keypress commands. They were super slow, at least in comparison with voice controls, and definitely when compared to neural links. But they were fail-safes, meant for emergencies.

"Let's see. Think, Yared. What did he say?" Thinking out loud helped me settle my nerves. "Most exo suits were built with a universal fail-safe, right? Just in case the pilot was in trouble. That way anyone could disengage the suit and rescue the pilot in an emergency. Soooo, if I press these two toggles, I think, and then hit these four in sequence, the suit should . . ."

Fwip.

"Yes!" I shouted as the HUD went dark and began to reboot. "Yared the Gr8, one! Weird series of unbelievable events, zero. I swear, if I find out Besa and the Ibis had anything to do with this practical joke, they'll be—"

I finally got a look at what I was wearing, and my mouth dropped open.

"—sorry."

It was the exo from Harar Station—the one in that abandoned research lab district. But how had . . . ?

New pilot registered. Emergency systems reset. Active scanners offline. Passive scanners charging at 42 percent. Comm module offline. One priority message queued. Play message?

As the bright green text scrolled in front of my face, a series of memories ran through my head like a slideshow. The exo coming online when I touched it. Me calling for help through the Radial when the scrappers swarmed. The shadow of a figure defending me as I lost consciousness. I'd thought it was the Ibis, but could it have been this old thing?

This was so weird. Once I figured out where I was and contacted someone to come get me, I was going to download the exo's memory core and figure out what happened. But first . . .

"System, disengage," I said. I was ready to get out of this antique.

Hostiles in the area. Unable to disengage.

I blinked. Hostiles in the area? "System, scan the area and call for help."

Active scanners charging at 58 percent. Comm module offline.

Oh yeah. This was going great. "Is there anything you can do? Can I at least see where we are? Jeez."

The visor tint cleared as the HUD finished rebooting. Finally, I could take stock of where I was and make a plan to get help. First things first, I'd have to get the scanners and the comm module back online. Then I would . . .

All thoughts in my head froze as I got my first look at my surroundings. I stood on the edge of a giant ring-shaped platform. Broken steel guardrails lined its edge in some spots, warped and twisted metal bending out and away, as if something massive had burst through them. When I peeked over the edge, empty space descended into darkness as the floor fell away into a giant bowl hundreds of meters deep, before flattening out into rough and uneven grounds covered in overgrown grassy furrows and what looked like tall pillars of scrap parts about twice as tall as me. Behind me, huge walls curved back and up to a transparent blue shield that sealed us in. Rows and rows of dented, melted, and sometimes completely missing seats lined the walls. Faded words stretched across a broken sign. It took me a moment to figure out what I was looking at, but when I did, I shook my head in confusion.

"Gibe Arena," I said. "But . . . I don't understand."

Something rumbled in the distance. A large shadow shifted down on the arena floor.

I gulped.

"Nope," I muttered, trying to figure out the exo's controls as I backed away. "System, scanner status!"

Active scanners engaged once reboot completes in three . . . two . . . one.

"Finally, you old piece of junk! Show me something! Thrusters, motor control, antigrav boots—don't you have any sort of propulsion system? How do you move? Wishful thinking? Okay, what's this . . . is that . . . ? There!"

I flipped a series of toggles, and an icon flashed on my HUD. It was a picture of a goat-like creature leaping upward, wickedly curved horns sticking out of its head.

"WALYA System online," a voice echoed inside my helmet.

"WALYA System?" I muttered aloud. "What is that? Whatever, I'll figure it out later. Here I come, Jemal!" I took a step . . . and then immediately yelped in surprise as my exo launched itself fifteen feet in the air. I closed my eyes, terrified of the brutal impact surely about to happen. But instead, I felt myself land gently.

"What . . . was . . . that?" I gasped, once my heartbeat had returned to normal. My arms flailed to keep me balanced. At least, until I realized I wasn't falling. Instead, the suit balanced itself, rocking back and forth. "Suit, what is the WALYA System?"

A holo-tutorial appeared in front of my helmet, demonstrating the suit's capabilities. An automated voice chirped in my ear. "Wingless Altitude Locomotive and Yeoman Armature—designed to navigate steep terrain and cover large stretches of ground with powerful, spring-loaded piston action. With superior balance and excellent speed, the

WALYA light-armored exoskeleton also excels at unarmed combat and is capable of utilizing multiple combat profiles. Current combat profile loaded: Sengis."

In the helmet's display, a miniature wireframe of the suit performed a leaping punch attack that sent three other opponents flying backward. I raised an eyebrow.

"WALYA System," I said again in disbelief. "I've never even heard of that. 'Spring-loaded'? That means no thrusters? No antigrav? What's next, fossil fuels? Is this retro-world?" I cautiously took another step, wincing as the legs creaked ominously. But to my surprise, nothing happened. In fact, the suit didn't even wobble. I experimented by purposely slipping my foot, and the suit responded instantly, shifting its weight until I could find another foothold. Hmm. That was cool, I guess. "WALYA, run scans. I need to find something to fix the comm module or we're never getting out of this . . . lovely establishment."

"Alert," the WALYA said. "Active scans commencing."

A bright cone of light emerged from the WALYA's chest armor and began to sweep the room. There were more of those towers. And . . . something else.

One of the shadowy lumps, what I thought was a pillar, shook itself. Six long, thin metal legs unfolded. Was that a . . . bot? It stood upright, a tall and slender drone with the head of a scrapper and the body of a praying mantis . . . if it was the size of a hoverbus. Suddenly, more scrappers rose into the air alongside it, buzzing around its body like flies. Their stasis stingers spit blue sparks.

The weird bot began to hum and vibrate loudly, and I felt the ledge beneath us shake. Dust fell and cracks appeared in the wall behind us.

When the scanner's light fell on it, the drone began to shriek.

CHAPTER NINE

The drone stalked forward. Its footsteps echoed through-out the dark, abandoned arena, the only light coming from the thin flashlights on my exo. From my view, it looked like a nightmare was emerging from the darkness. I gulped in fear as the drone stepped into view.

Two arms dangled at its side, while a third swept through the air, gathering up scrappers and pressing them to its torso, where they buzzed and rattled like disgusting bug magnets. It used three of its legs to walk. I couldn't help but think it reminded me of a murderous tripod, hungry for a multitalented and devilishly handsome prince.

(Sorry, I brag when I'm terrified. Besa says I need to work on that.)

(I hoped she was okay.)

The thought of Besa shot through me like a burst of adrenaline. I had to move. If that thing caught me, chances were it wouldn't want to talk about the weather. The way it had shrieked, and the way its eyestalks swiveled and peered into every shadow—no, that thing was *hunting* me.

I turned the exo and sprinted toward the back of the platform, sliding behind a pile of broken seats that must've fallen from the rows above. I closed my eyes and tried to calm my ragged breathing. After a few moments, I strained to listen. I didn't dare ask the WALYA to scan again, even though it would update my HUD with the drone's position. I counted to ten, then slowly, carefully, peeked around my hiding spot.

The drone had paused a few meters away from the platform. It just . . . stood there. What was it waiting for? I didn't have to wait long for the answer. A scrapper bot floated by, bumping into the platform. The drone struck like a bolt of lightning. It snagged the scrapper out of mid-air and pressed it to its frame, then turned and began to stride away. The scrapper wiggled for a few moments, its movements growing more sluggish with every second, until it stopped moving completely.

I shivered. Was that thing . . . absorbing the scrappers? That was creepy. Its knifelike legs stepped over the ditches and rubble dotting the arena floor with ease. As it moved deeper into the shadows and disappeared from sight, I realized just how tall it really was.

A few minutes later, I stepped out of my hiding spot. "WALYA," I whispered, "what was that?"

"Database corrupted. Rebuild currently in progress. However, there is an eighty-nine percent probability that the target is a Nefisati-class drone. Designed to manage, repair, and recycle scrapper bots and their locust counterparts, Nefisatis have higher-level programming algorithms. They are extremely territorial. Recommendation: Avoid and locate a communications module. Once located, the WALYA System can repair internal comm systems and connect with unknown pilot interface."

Unknown pilot interface? I was confused for a moment, until I realized WALYA was referring to my Radial. "You can fix it? How?"

"If a communications module can be located, unknown pilot interface and internal comm systems can be repaired."

Was it just me, or did the WALYA have a bit of an attitude? Maybe it hated repeating itself. Regardless, now we had a plan. I just had to locate a comm module. "Where can I find one?"

WALYA almost sounded regretful as it responded. "Unknown. It is possible human negligence has resulted in component disposal in inappropriate locations. Inconvenient for the planet, convenient for repair purposes. Scan recommended."

Okay, yeah, this exo definitely had an attitude. Did it just criticize humans for not recycling?

"Start scans," I said, slightly distracted by this rattling noise that had started up in the distance. I shuddered. The sooner we could find a comm module, the sooner I could call in a proper rescue and escape this horrifying arena of gloom and doom.

"Extended active scans commencing. Please note, extended scans cannot be terminated until process is completed."

"Wait!" I said suddenly, remembering what happened the last time. A bright cone of light, more powerful than before, shot out of the exo. It rotated, sweeping the area, and when it reached the farthest corner of the arena, a shadow shifted and shrieked.

"Shut it off, shut it off!" I shouted.

"Please note . . ." the WALYA began again. I whirled around in frustration, trying to get back to my hiding place, but it was too late. Nefisati came lunging out of the shadows, so fast I barely had time to react. I sidestepped—well, I tried to. Maybe if I was in a Meshenitai exo or something newer, I would've avoided the attack. But the WALYA's older system just couldn't move that fast. Nefisati's third arm sliced down like a humongous sword, slamming into the platform behind me and clipping me on the shoulder. I went tumbling to the shadowy arena floor.

CRASH!

I landed on one of the strange pillars and slid down the side of it, tumbling head over heels to the ground. The arms and legs of the WALYA got tangled in something. It took several seconds to free myself. Whatever it was, it looked like a thin metal sheet. I grabbed it and held it to my chest, covering the cone of light from the scans. I wobbled as I tried to get my bearings, still slightly dazed from the fall. That was going to hurt in the morning. Or the evening. What time was it? And what was that weird rattling noise?

Nefisati's shriek echoed throughout the arena. In my helmet, the sound popped and hissed through the speakers.

I shakily returned the WALYA to its feet. "Suit, turn on night vision," I whispered. Nothing happened. "Suit, turn on infrared. Or heat vision. Anything!"

No use.

Something flashed in the darkness. I retreated back to the giant pillar. It was my only landmark in the darkness. Hopefully once the scan finished, we could escape. If only the strange rattling would go away. Instead, it grew louder. Almost as if it was . . .

I looked up, searching the pillar. There, at the top, Nefisati's terrifying face loomed out of the darkness. Triangular and rusted, with bits of scrapper parts clinging like it had just finished feeding, the drone screeched.

Scrappers flooded out of the pillar.

No, not a pillar. An assembly hive—the largest scrapper hive I'd ever seen.

I ran.

The WALYA galloped through the shadowy arena, crashing through small towers of what I NOW REALIZED weren't piles of junk, but scrapper assembly hives. This is where the drones built themselves! But why so many? And why were the hives so huge? The ones back on Harar Station were half the size of these giants.

I knocked over another creepy stack of partially built drones and stumbled into a relatively clear space. The exo nearly tripped over a tangled braid of wires leading to a glowing crack in the wall. The scrappers were in the process of building a new hive over the crack. A secret exit, maybe? Before I could follow it, a cloud of scrappers erupted out of another assembly hive in front of me.

I skidded to a stop and yanked the controls left, sending the WALYA spinning in a whirling cloud of dust, clipping another tower on the way. "Sorry!" I shouted to the angry scrappers that came humming out of the rubble. "Still learning how to pilot this thing."

We went left, then right, then left again, finally stopping at a larger rocky outcropping that poked out of the arena floor. I let my head fall against the inside of my helmet, sucking down oxygen as I tried to get my heart to stop racing. This was ridiculous! Murderous insect-drones, a creepy robot overlord that could sneak up on me like a ghost, and a super-old exo with incredible dance moves.

What next, a pop quiz?

The outcropping I was hiding beneath began to crumble.

"Oh no," I said, exhausted beyond belief. "WALYA, how long until the scan is finished?"

"Scan is seventy percent complete," the system answered.

Great. I just had to hold out for a little bit longer. Then hopefully we'd have a way out of this place.

The outcropping shuddered as a crack began to run up the rock, splitting it in half. Pieces fell to the floor with a crash. Two large serrated legs stabbed through, shredding the column into chunks. The largest scrapper I'd ever seen scuttled out.

It had to be at least the size of Besa in her full Guardian mode, with black shining metal instead of the dull gray of the smaller drones. It had three stasis stingers instead of just the one, and two large spoon-like arms flexed. Glowing balls of energy fizzled at the ends.

I sighed. That wasn't a rocky column I'd been hiding behind. It was an upgrade cocoon. And those spoon-like arms? You guessed it. Stasis catapults.

The drone crawled across the floor. Several more upgraded scrappers shook themselves clear of the rubble and followed.

"Suit, identify those unknown things," I said.

"Reminder: Extended active scans are ongoing," the WALYA said. "Reminder: Database remains offline. Last database update: ten thousand, seven hundred, and sixty-two days ago. Closest approximation, according to current records: the locust, a flying insectoid robot capable of devouring kilometers of vegetation in hours."

Right, the locust bots it had mentioned earlier. I gulped. "Flying?"

The drone nearest to me shivered. Metallic wings unfurled and began to beat as it lifted into the air. The others soon followed.

I groaned. "Flying. Got it. Time to see what the WALYA is made of, I guess. Suit, designate larger drones as locust-bots, soldier class."

"Database updated. Sync still required."

"Yeah, yeah. I know, you're old."

Six or seven drones hummed around me, their stasis catapults ready to attack. The green balls of energy crackled as the drones inched closer.

"Fine," I said. "You want a fight? Say less." I licked my lips and flexed my fingers. I had no idea how strong those locust drones were, but if they were more dangerous than the scrappers, I was in trouble. Hopefully I could take out one, maybe two, and then avoid the rest while the scans finished up.

Suddenly, three of the locust drones lunged forward, two in front of me and one behind me. Each appeared as a glowing red dot on my helmet's HUD. I waited until they were seconds away from turning me into a pile of ash, then jumped, intending to leap over them and try to escape back into the maze of assembly hives. Instead . . .

"Whoa!" I shouted as the WALYA sprang nearly a dozen meters into the air. We soared above the locusts, above the scrappers, and even higher than many of the assembly hives. For a few brief seconds, I actually forgot about the danger I was in. This was incredible! Like, the closest thing to flying.

At least, until we began to fall. Fast.

A shrieking wail filled my helmet. After a moment, I realized it was coming from me, not one of the alerts on my HUD. My fingers flew over the control toggles, trying to activate any sort of protection that would keep my face from turning into chewed injera. But it was no use. I couldn't find anything!

The HUD flashed to let me know the ground was approaching.

"I know!" I shouted. Finally, I squeezed my eyes shut, not wanting to see the moment of collision.

WHUMPH.

A jarring impact rocked the WALYA. Not the bone-crushing shock I was expecting, however. I opened one eye to see . . . well, I was still alive, for one. That was awesome. Never can complain about that. But even more impressive was the perfect circle of destruction radiating outward, with me—and the WALYA—at its center.

Shattered scrappers, toppled assembly hives, and dust radiated outward for at least twenty meters. And the WALYA . . .

The exo knelt in a crouch, one massive arm plunged into the ground in a fist-shaped crater. My jaw dropped. "No way," I said. "WALYA, what sort of unarmed combat do you have?"

"The WALYA System's current combat profile is designed for high-velocity, high-impact encounters," the WALYA's AI answered. "Current combat profile is designated as Sengis."

"Teff of the saints," I whispered, staring at the devastation. "You've got some moves."

"Indeed," it said, and I rolled my eyes. "More importantly, extended active scans have been completed."

"And?"

"A module to repair communications and unknown pilot interface has been located and marked on your HUD. Activity in the area is minimal, though unknown exoskeleton suits are present. Recommend proceeding with speed and caution."

I nodded. Finally, some good news! If I could get my Radial working and the WALYA's comm systems functional as well, we could tap into a secure channel to call for help. I could practically feel my bed back on Harar Station calling me. I was going to stay under the covers until next Enkutatash.

"Apologies for interrupting the puzzling human behavior of daydreaming while in danger, but . . . danger."

I didn't have a chance to comment on the WALYA's sarcastic tone, because something rustled in the darkness to my left. I whirled the WALYA around and cocked its arms back, ready to spring into action.

Nefisati emerged from the gloom.

Nefisati faced me in the middle of the abandoned arena. A cloud of scrappers hummed high in the air above our heads, their stasis stingers glowing at full strength. The weird blue lights partially illuminated the space.

Assembly hive towers dotted the arena floor, like we were standing in what a robot considered a forest. More shadows moved in the darkness between the pillars. I gulped. You ever get the feeling that things you couldn't see were watching you, and there were a lot of them? Yeah. Creepy.

But what was even stranger was the fact that, despite the eerie landscape, there was something sort of familiar about the place. I just couldn't put my finger on what was nagging me.

Suddenly, the giant bot lunged forward, slicing downward, and only a knee-jerk reaction sent the WALYA jumping out of the way. Right. I had to focus. Impending doom and all that.

"Okay, listen," I said. "No offense, and don't get me wrong—I would love to hang out—but I really do need to get going. Have to get back to my family. You seem like a real family . . . bug. What with those terrifying knives you've got for arms. Perfect for, you know, hugging. And stabbing. But mostly hugging, I hope."

SLICE.

I barely dodged another lunging attack, and this time, I didn't waste a second. I turned and sprinted down a zigzagging row of hive towers, turning at random, until I was deep in the middle of the arena. I could hear Nefisati chasing me. The giant bot's tripod legs sounded like guillotines slamming into the ground. Every so often, a tower would shatter as the creature crashed into it, and clouds of scrappers would erupt into the air, humming and sparking as their stasis stingers brushed against one another. The air above me crackled.

Nefisati shrieked a challenge. The drone barreled into me, emerging from a shadow on my left to hurl me to the ground, knocking several other hives down in the process. I grunted in pain as I tumbled head over heels. The sturdy frame of the WALYA was the only thing that kept me from serious injury.

"Damage?" I asked. I crawled behind a partially destroyed hive and peeked around.

"It appears you've suffered several contusions and possibly a concussion. There is also a medium-length bruise running along your leg that may require further analysis."

"Not me," I snapped. "Damage to you. Are you hurt?"

The WALYA paused. In the silence, I heard Nefisati shriek again as it searched for me. "Systems operating well within recommended efficiencies," the exo finally said.

I peeked around. The scrappers from the destroyed hives were clustered in the air, several meters above Nefisati's head. Their stasis stingers were pulsing. From here it almost looked like an alarm was going off.

Suddenly, Nefisati lunged and plucked a scrapper out of the air, pressing it to its carapace. There was that flash of light again. A group of scrappers began to pulse their stingers faster. They buzzed away, keeping their distance. It almost looked like . . .

"That creature isn't managing them," I said, realization washing over me. "It's *harvesting* them. Look, it's using the stasis stingers to recharge its own power supplies. The scrappers build their hives here, and Nefisati collects their stingers and charges itself. Probably since it's trapped in here and can't get to a normal power source."

"That is . . . possible," the WALYA said begrudgingly.

I smirked. "Don't get mad because you were wrong once."

"Once," the exo sniffed. Can exos sniff? Was it a hiss of static? More on that later, when I had the time to research. "Recommendation: A plan of action for escape and systems repair is in order . . . now that the score counting is done."

Some people—or sentient exoskeletons—really can't handle being wrong.

"I'm working on it," I said, watching Nefisati stalk the shadows. "I think I have an idea."

"Wonderful."

I ignored the WALYA. "See, the funny thing about power supplies? They have to be connected to work."

This was going to be close. There was only a fraction of a second when Nefisati would be vulnerable. I'd have to time it so that I was preparing the strike even before the opportunity presented itself.

Typical Yared the Gr8 move.

A scrapper emerged from a hive, and I watched Nefisati's head swivel toward it.

It was time.

A scythe-like hand sliced toward the scrapper. At the same time, I sent the WALYA leaping into the air. Five meters. Ten. Fifteen. I was soaring above the arena floor, silent as a shadow. Nefisati snagged the scrapper and brought it to its carapace, right where a narrow slit ran from its head all the way down its torso. For an instant—a brief moment in time—the carapace opened. And as Nefisati moved to absorb the energy from the scrapper's stasis stinger, I—we—struck.

"Sengis PUNCH!" I shouted.

I could feel it. Just for a second, the WALYA and I were on the same page, almost as if we'd been working together forever. Teammates.

The WALYA drove its fist into the inner structure of Nefisati like a hammer. The drone shrieked as sparks flew and smoke poured out of its chest. Scrappers flew off it like birds erupting from a tree. Nefisati collapsed into a twitching heap.

I landed in a heroic crouch, keeping a safe distance as the giant bot grew still. "That . . . was . . . awesome," I huffed.

I stood and watched as hundreds of scrappers descended to reclaim their stasis energy.

"Don't take this the wrong way, WALYA, but I don't want to face anything as strong as that ever again. No more fights for a while. Let's just go get the comm module and be on our way."

"So," the WALYA said as it charted a path up and over the arena wall, "about that . . ."

Automated Voice: Playing holofeed.

nanoL0gic: Welcoooooooome to another incredible edition of *epiCast*! Coming to you live from our holostream studio in the Jupiter Colony Academy. We have to again give another big shout-out to our partners at neAR Glasses, *the* definitive source for augmented reality glasses this side of the nebula.

nanoL0gic: And now let's jump into some questions. Hello! Welcome to the stream! What's your name, and what's your question?

Jess_E: Hi, nano. My name's Jesse, and I was wondering how they're choosing the arenas for the different match types. Thanks!

nanoL0gic: Great question, Jesse! Perfect time to cut away to a flyover. Get ready, folks—the opening round of the Royal Trials is here, and with it, the debut of the galaxy's most anticipated new addition: Control! Twenty bases, sixty-four players, tons of chaos. And with that many players, you just knew new maps had to happen, too, right?

nanoL0gic: This round is being played at the newly

constructed Titan Arena, a re-creation of a low-orbital farm circling Jupiter's largest moon. Players will have to navigate craters the size of lakes, massive dunes, and mysterious ruins left from an abandoned terraforming project. As this is the first round, the location was selected by game officials. The next arena, however, will be chosen by the highest-ranking team at the end of the game.

nanoL0gic: And you know the stakes, folks—points are scored for occupying bases. But! Bonus points can be earned for taking out opposing players. The top players with the highest point totals at the end of the game move on to the next round, while the lower half are going home. So cheer on your faves, folks, and be sure to link with the *epiCast* holo-feed if you want up-to-the-second updates on the Royal Trials.

nanoL0gic: Uh-oh, it looks . . . Yep, folks, we're moments away from starting the opening round. We'll see you afterward right here, on *epiCast*!

Round One

Match Type: Control

Teams will battle for dominance over control points. The longer a team maintains a point, the more their score will increase. Teams can also increase their scores by defeating opposing players, albeit by lesser amounts. Control points will spawn randomly throughout the arena.

Special Items:

- *Shield*
- *Score Multiplier*
- *** Error: Unknown item***

Ready?

Begin!

CHAPTER TEN

The family that trains together remains together.

That was Mom's favorite thing to say when she'd have Besa drag me out of bed at 0400 ST during the last few months on Harar Station. She'd shove a juice bulb in my hand and then take me to the training simulator, where adults would be loud for no reason. I'm talking *every*one was shouting so loud the neighbors in the next star system over could probably hear it. And I do mean everyone . . . Dad, Mom, Uncle Moti, even Besa. The training lasted for nearly an hour, and you know what? I've never seen anyone get under Uncle Moti's skin the way my dad did.

"Come on, *General*," my dad taunted. The Emperor feinted with the long stick he carried—what he called a quarterstaff, and I called unfair, and what Besa called a chew toy—and skipped back when Uncle Moti tried to bat it aside with his own weapon. "Leader of the Burning Legion. Fierce defender of the crown prince and heir. Sole operator of the holo-tainment center. Show us your moves."

Wait. Did I mention we were actually *fighting*? Not exo training or flight training. Fighting. Apparently, it was a family tradition. And now that we were all together, every other week Uncle Moti and Dad and Mom and I would head to one of the Meshenitai training modules and battle it out for bragging rights (and sometimes extra sambusas, let's be honest).

I'd just gotten finished working out with Besa and I was off my game. (It happens to the best.) None of my attacks landed on Besa, and she wasn't even in full Guardian mode! So they made the two of us take a break, and meanwhile, two out of the top three warriors in Axum sparred with each other.

(In case you're wondering, Dad and Uncle Moti said Mom was better than *both* of them. They were sparring for a chance to challenge her to a match.)

It was incredible to watch Dad and Uncle Moti fight. I mean, I knew Uncle Moti was good. He'd worked with me all the time. But what I didn't know was how good he was when he was truly challenged. When he turned into General Moti Berihun. That's when he *really* got loose.

And Dad was no pushover, either. He sent attack after attack at Uncle Moti, swiping left and right, spinning his staff with a flourish as he tried to get past his opponent's defenses, talking trash the whole time.

"Surely Axum's greatest hero, my own former combat tutor, can defeat his old student?" Dad lunged forward, then backpedaled when Uncle Moti parried and feinted. "Or did you teach a certain prince too much?"

I grinned. Now I knew where I got my swagger from. When I glanced at Mom, she was leaning on her own quarterstaff and rolling her eyes. She wasn't even concerned that either of them might get hurt! In fact, she met my gaze and winked, then pointed at the two men as if to say, *Watch closely.*

Dad sent attack after attack at Uncle Moti, and I got a little worried. Uncle Moti wasn't doing anything other than dodging and retreating! Where was the offense? Had he lost a step?

Finally, Dad launched a blistering attack. I'm talking left, right, head, feet . . . his quarterstaff was everywhere! Even Besa looked concerned. Uncle Moti kept backing up, kept his guard up, but never tried to respond. Dad jumped high in the air—so high I held my breath—landing with a two-handed power attack that would've crushed a bone had it landed.

Except Uncle Moti wasn't there.

Flick.

Dad's staff went flying across the training room.

Flick.

Dad tumbled to the floor.

Whoosh.

The tip of Uncle Moti's staff hovered, perfectly still, inches from Dad's throat. No one moved. I held my breath. Then Uncle Moti's lips quivered, and Dad's cheeks ballooned out, and the two collapsed into helpless laughter. I looked over at Mom, and she rolled her eyes and muttered something under her breath that sounded suspiciously like *grown children.*

"Yared," Dad called after taking a moment to regain his breath. "What lesson can you take from this?"

I groaned. I should've known. There was always a lesson somewhere. Those things were everywhere, like flies. Huge flies. With mustaches, because why not.

"Um, don't jump and attack?" I guessed.

Dad laughed and clapped Uncle Moti on the shoulder, who was also chuckling. "That is probably the second-most-important lesson, I'll grant you. Especially against someone as skilled as this man. No, there's another lesson here, and the general demonstrated it beautifully. Moti?"

Uncle Moti stood, offered an arm, and helped the Emperor of Axum to his feet. Then he walked over to me and rested a hand on my shoulder. "Patience. You must not let yourself get rattled when facing an opponent of unknown strength, or someone who just seems to have your number on a particular day. Watch. Wait. Observe. Learn. And when it's time—"

The quarterstaff whipped off the ground, twirled in the air, and landed perfectly vertical behind Uncle Moti's back as he caught it and dropped into his fighting stance.

"—strike!"

"You've got to be kidding."

I glared at my HUD as the location marker the WALYA had set blinked. According to the map, the comm module I needed was right in front of us. And that was the problem.

"When you said you found a comm module," I said quietly, "I assumed you meant salvage. Something no one would see us taking. I didn't realize I would have to BREAK INTO A ROYAL TRIALS MATCH!"

"Apologies," the WALYA said, "for not putting limitations on saving your life."

I bit off my next statement as a group of exos stomped by. I glanced around to make sure no one could hear me arguing with the WALYA. We stood on the edge of a large grassy field where dozens and dozens of exos gathered beneath the shadow of a massive orbital platform. Humans and drones alike sped this way and that, organizing the chaos and transmitting instructions. A huge medibot lurked at the end of the field next to a giant banner.

Royal Trials Opening Round.

The banner dissolved into a picture of another arena—this one was newer than the Gibe Arena I'd just escaped from, and it was called the Titan Arena. How did I know? Because the branding was everywhere. Drones stamped with the Titan logo buzzed by. The field was littered with holo-ads that offered the newest AR glasses, or a stat booster, or an energy paste that apparently you didn't eat but smeared on your forehead. Don't ask me.

It was ridiculous. It was . . . It . . .

Teff of the saints, I wanted to play so bad. It was everything I thought it would be and more. The energy, the excitement, the obstacles and opponents. That could've been me getting ready. That *should've* been me getting ready.

"All scans indicate that the comm module is unclaimed and inside the contest grounds," the WALYA was saying. "Retrieval can commence once game officials are notified of your presence."

I hesitated. "What will happen to the Royal Trials?"

"With heightened response times as a direct result of pirate alerts on the Sol-Luna newsvids, and the presence of the imperial heir, the likelihood of the Royal Trials being canceled is very high."

No. That couldn't happen. I thought about how hard I'd trained for the game, then multiplied that effort and sleepless nights and the time and cost of even just traveling to Old Earth—how could I be the reason it was ended? There had to be another way.

"What if we tried to find a different comm module?"

The WALYA fell silent as it—I guess—calculated the answer. Then it spoke. "Calculations indicate the probability of successfully fixing communications and signaling a rescue are above seventy percent if the present comm module is retrieved. If it isn't, or if a comm module not of Axum design is substituted, probabilities drop to zero point seven percent." After a second's pause, it added: "You are of course free to use your own calculations."

Zingers. Straight zingers.

But the exo, attitude or not, did have a point. I could try something else, maybe hope to get lucky with salvage or a friendly face, but the odds were more likely I'd never find anything useful. I needed that module. But canceling the game was like a punch to the gut. If only . . .

"What if . . . ?" I started to ask, licking my lips as the sheer audacity of what I was about to say nearly overwhelmed me. "What if I didn't let anyone know I was here? What if I entered the game, searched for the comm module, maybe punched an exo or two, and then left? We'd still have the comm module and the Royal Trials could continue."

"That—" the WALYA said after a moment.

"Makes sense, right?"

"—actually has a negative probability of being successful." I nodded. "That's good."

"It is the opposite of good. It is . . . such a foolhardy human thing to propose."

"Well, here's the thing about Yared the Gr8: I'm the hardiest fool you'll ever meet." I took a quick glance around to make sure no one was watching, then hopped the fence to the arena and walked as if I belonged there. Because I did. "Come on," I said, "let's go be sneaky."

The orbital platform reminded me of the Ibis's orbital farm actually, except the facility had been upgraded and modified to accommodate the Royal Trials. Hundreds of exos packed the giant space. Server-bots floated around offering refreshments, while mechanic drones hummed overhead on their way to perform a tune-up request. People laughed, shouted, stared, and pointed, and if it had been my first time, I definitely would've panicked. But I'd been in tons of launch lobbies—though not as fancy as this—back on Addis Prime. In fact, ten days ago if you would've told me I'd be in the opening round of the Royal Trials, I would've flipped. This is where I'd wanted to be, and what I'd wanted to do. But priorities change—now I wanted to escape as quickly as possible. If I could just get that comm module . . .

"Watch it!" Someone bumped the WALYA as I paused in the entrance. I stumbled back.

A boy in a silver exo glared at me and muttered something under his breath. Two other exos followed him, the same models but in a navy-blue color. The three gathered at the opposite end of the platform. I shook my head and turned back around.

"Hey, kid, you okay?"

I looked up to see another exo standing in front of me. A newer model, way sleeker and cooler than the WALYA I was in. (No offense to the WALYA, but we both knew the deal.) The visor faded from black tint to transparent, and an older girl peered out, curiosity written on her face. Her exo was orange and silver, with holographic graffiti circling the thrusters on her leg armor. It looked pretty cool. Two more matching exos waited a short distance behind her.

"Yeah, I'm fine," I said, still struggling with how to get to the comm module.

But the girl mistook my silence for fear and popped off her helmet. "Ignore them. Money can buy you everything but manners." She shook her head. "First time? It can get pretty overwhelming in the launch lobby."

I couldn't exactly tell this nice stranger that I was trying to figure out a way to steal the grand prize of the match. She would report me! So I just nodded, and the girl smiled. "Figured as much. Listen, you wouldn't be here if you hadn't earned it."

Oh, if only you knew, I thought.

"Diarra," she said, introducing herself.

"Ya—" I began to say, then paused. "Haji," I said, using my friend's name from back on Addis Prime. Just in case. "Nice to meet you."

Diarra smiled. "Ignore those guys. I think everyone's a little nervous," she continued. "A lot riding on today's outcome."

"What do you mean?"

She dropped into a crouch next to me. I couldn't help but admire the absolute silence of her armor. No squeak, no scrape, no screech. Like, not a peep. Just a smooth, well-oiled, high-powered, and *new* piece of equipment. Again . . . no shade to the WALYA, but every time I took a step it sounded like Besa that time she got stuck in Uncle Moti's stove. Just a lot of squealing and screeching.

"You didn't hear? We're doing live fights," Diarra whispered in a sly voice.

Two days ago, if someone told me that, I would have jumped for the moons. Now . . . not so much. Live fights?

That meant actual combat, not augmented reality weapons that did virtual damage. Exo suits could be seriously damaged in a live fight. Maybe I should've found a game admin to help me out. I didn't want the WALYA to—

Just then, a series of lights began to flash around the launch zone, and an automated voice instructed all teams to queue up. Diarra patted me on the back, stood, and rejoined her friends.

"Good luck, newbie!" she shouted before putting her helmet back on. "I hope you don't lose!"

"Me too," I muttered as the orbital platform's bay doors began to close in preparation for launch. Too late for second-guessing . . . The game had begun.

Here are Yared's Rules of Free-for-All Gaming. Doesn't matter if it's a battle royale, Trios, king of the hill, control, or any other game type where it's every player for themselves. I call them Yared's ABCs. Ready? Okay, listen close:

Always Be cMoving.

. . .

The *c* is silent.

. . .

Okay, fine, it doesn't really work as an acronym, but you get the picture. Never stand still or hover in place. It makes you an easy target. That goes for when you're in-game and out. Trust me. If you bounced around different schools on Addis Prime like I did, you'd know how to keep an eye peeled. Bullies and spawn campers have the same energy.

As soon as the orbital platform opened its cargo bay doors over the arena, I launched myself into the air. Twisting into a spiral, I tucked the WALYA's arms against its body to put on a burst of speed, then took a brief glance behind me. A flood of players followed. I frowned. I wasn't trying to get taken out as soon as I landed. Were the other players trying to pick us off in midair, or did they think I knew something about the map? That's another way to tell experienced players from those who are new to the game. New players will head straight for the closest ground they can find, while wiser players will pick the terrain that best suits their play style.

SHINK.

A piece of armor bounced off the WALYA's shoulder, and I swerved left, narrowly avoiding an exo as it tumbled wildly, smoke pouring from a broken thruster. A few meters to my right, two more exos exchanged wild punches as they fell. A third dropped like a hammer on both, one foot on each back. Then the group rocketed out of sight.

I shook my head. Almost forgot my own rule. "C'mon, Yared," I said. "Keep your head on a swivel." If you're looting a treasure box, do it fast. Too many ambushes have been set at unopened loot troves. If you have to move in the open (and you shouldn't; always find cover), do it quickly. Sprint. Keep low and keep going. That's the key.

And as I fell from the sky, that's exactly what I did.

Exos can't fly. Not exactly. Too heavy and unwieldy. (Unless you were Uncle Moti's friend Kamali, but then, her exo also transformed into a bunamech, so you can't really use her as an example.) But the rockets built into their leg armor, what we called thrusters, had enough boosting power to send pilots across short distances at great speed, including into the air. An experienced player would use them during the opening-round drop to pick out a good landing spot or to take out unsuspecting players before they themselves could land. I've done it to other players in plenty of games.

CLANG.

The air whooshed out of my lungs as someone collided with me. I peeked over my shoulder. Never mind. Someones. Two exos were following me, and from the way they spread out and sped up, they were trying to take me out. The nerve. I muttered something Besa would probably ground me for saying, then quickly glanced at the arena. It was getting closer and closer with every second.

Titan had been designed to look like an abandoned mining colony. A circular map was divided into four sections.

Pretty good job, actually. Giant orbital launchers—remnants of Earth's efforts to get supplies spaceborne—floated just above the ground in the northwest corner. A large star-shaped recreation building with scorch marks along the roof and walls lay half-buried in the sand in the southeast. The center of the map was scattered with a maze of empty escape shuttles, and a behemoth of a cargo transport lay partially broken in the southwest section. A few towers, some abandoned residential living units, and Titus was the perfect arena for today's match. Now I just had to figure out where the comm module item pickup was going to spawn and grab it first.

Something gleamed on the ground below. A shiny object was being carried by a drone between a pair of grounded shuttles, just over the top of a field of wild teff. It floated a few meters in one direction, then turned and retraced its path, its quad rotors bending the grain plants down as it passed over them.

Item drop!

I landed in an awkward roll, hopped to my feet, and sent the WALYA sprinting ahead in bounding, turf-eating strides. I had to get there first. If someone else collected the pickup before I did . . .

A blast of air nearly knocked me off my feet as three exos blew by me. I skidded to a stop near the partially open door of a cargo shuttle, confused. It looked like the armored suits had wings . . . but exos couldn't fly. Right? What was going on? I stepped into the shuttle's shadow and peeked out.

The lead exo spun about in midair and landed, facing me as it skidded backward. One hand was outstretched to pluck the item from the drone. Not going to lie, it was a pretty cool move.

"Got it," I heard the exo say. I grimaced as I recognized the suit and the voice inside it. It was the rude boy from the orbital. So his exo was just as powerful as it looked. Teff of the saints, why couldn't anything ever be simple and straightforward? And to make matters worse . . .

His partners swooped in and dropped by his side. This was looking bad—I should've run immediately, but I had to see what they'd picked up.

"What is it?" a high, scratchy voice asked.

The third exo leaned closer, only to jump backward nearly three meters when the leader snapped at him through his helmet. "Don't even think about it. Besides, it's just a little speed boost consumable. Worthless—we're fast enough as it is."

I sighed with relief. Not the comm module. Fine, now I could wait for them to leave and then continue my own search.

"WALYA," I whispered to my HUD, "scan for the comm module item pickup."

"Unable to scan," the suit said through my helmet speakers. "Possibility of shielding."

I groaned. The game admins probably didn't want people camping for power-ups, so they were blocking them from exo scanners. This is why we couldn't have nice things. "Fine," I rasped, "scan for miniature power sources, like the drones carrying power-up items might use. They should move in repeating patterns."

"Scanning."

I peeked around the side of the shuttle again and watched as the three players bickered over where to go next. Even though this was supposed to be a solo match, seeing other players team up wasn't that odd. Not fair, but also not odd. I'd have to try and avoid them—and other similar groups.

"Scans finished. Three possible targets located. Two are moving faster than the third—possibility that their cargo has been removed."

I just had to hope the comm module was with that third drone. "Mark the slower target."

An icon appeared on my HUD. When I peeked around the shuttle again, the three exos were gone. Good. I charted a path through the overgrown shuttle yard and across the map to the icon's location: a lookout post atop a hill near the old residential living units. Keeping low and avoiding as many other players as I could, I made my way across the map.

Once, I nearly ran into a group of exos who were stalking two others already locked in a duel. It was the trio from before—they waited until the duelists were occupied, then swooped down on them, attacking with bright energy wings extending from their shoulders. I shook my head. They were too powerful. Better to avoid them.

Finally, I reached a hill with the lookout post. It was nothing more than a bunker with two large entrances and a wide interior. Nearly impossible to hold by myself. I just needed . . . there it was!

A drone puttered through the air, bobbing slightly as it traveled in a circle midway up the hill. A conical cylinder with a picture of a satellite antenna dangled beneath it. I grinned fiercely. The comm module! I started to run up the hill just as a loud siren split the air.

"Warning! Game ending in ten minutes. Warning! Game ending in ten minutes!"

That didn't matter. I just had to grab the comm module. If the drone returned to its base while still holding it, I'd lose it forever. All I had to do was wait until the drone circled around to the backside of the hill, stealthily retrieve the comm module, and disappear in the chaos of the match's end. No problem. No problem at—

"Hostiles detected," the WALYA said just as three shining exos flashed by overhead.

*   *   *

Ten minutes until the game ended and the drone returned to its base. I had to grab the comm module . . . while defending myself against three players who wanted to take me out, all piloting newer and more powerful exos.

Easy-peasy lemon-squeezy.

Right.

"Spread out . . . he's around here somewhere."

I crept up the hill under the base, checking out the lines of sight and trying to anticipate where the other players would attack. Tall teff and leafy vines crawled up the sides of the structure, snaking in and out of the two entrances. I shook my head. Trying to predict anything was impossible. I just had to stay on my toes.

"Hostiles detected."

The WALYA flagged the enemy exos coming in from the north. I couldn't see them yet because they were blocked by the hill, but the WALYA could sense them somehow. Red rectangles appeared on my HUD, growing brighter as the attackers grew closer. I climbed up the final meters of the hill, hugging the wall at the rear of the base and peeking inside the lookout post. The interior was a dozen meters across on all sides, barely enough room to get a good running start.

"Hostiles approaching," the WALYA repeated, but this

time it added, "Recommend observing, instead of the typical human response of a chaotic plunge."

"Hard to observe as I'm getting my faceshield stomped," I muttered.

"That observation style is not recommended."

I sighed. Between Besa and now the WALYA, I'd had my fill of snarky machines. Maybe Nefasati would take me back.

Just then, three exos roared over the base, the blast of wind following them nearly ripping the flimsy wooden supports out of the ground. I braced myself and stuck my head out, watching as they swooped and dove in midair. The WALYA placed an orange circle around them to go with the red highlighted square. The longer I studied each exo, the more the orange circle filled, until all were solid in color.

"Observation complete. New combat profile detected. Analyzing combat profile."

I shrugged and peeked at the timer. Eight minutes. The drone was circling the front of the hill and on its way to the rear. If I could hold on for just a little bit longer, then I'd be able to—

"Hostile attack!"

The WALYA's warning barely gave me enough time to whirl around and throw up my hands. One of the exos had split off from the group and was trying to get in a sneak attack while my back was turned. How had they spotted me?

The exo suit the other player wore was smaller than the WALYA, but its arms were long and skinny. Its energy wings ended in bladelike pinion feathers that shimmered with an orangish glow. The boy knifed toward me and sliced downward. The impact rattled the WALYA, and I stumbled back. By the time I regained my balance and swung a balled metal fist, the exo had already zipped back out the base and was out of sight.

"Too slow, loser!" a voice crackled through my helmet speakers. "Just give up already. I'm surprised you made it this long in that old piece of junk."

I gritted my teeth but didn't respond. Not even a few hours ago, I was calling the WALYA the same thing, but after piloting it for a bit, it was starting to grow on me. And hearing someone *else* talk trash about *my* exo was infuriating. It was like the little sibling rule—or what I assumed to be the rule, as Besa was the closest thing I had to a sibling— no one was allowed to insult them but me.

"Hostile attacks incoming."

This time I was prepared. I leapt to the side of the base entrance as another one of the winged exos zoomed in. I spun around in a tight circle with both fists extended. The exo's own momentum carried it into my spinning punch, and it crashed into the wooden wall opposite me. A red flickering X highlighted it on my display. One down.

"You little jerk," the leader said. The WALYA flagged him high in the sky above us, circling like a bird of prey. "Some moves still left in that rusty bucket. Joseph was always impatient. But you forgot about Ama."

Something slammed into my back. I flew out of the base, tumbling halfway down the hill until a large moss-covered boulder stopped my descent with a shuddering impact.

"Hnng," I groaned.

"Alert: Damage detected. Auto-repair engaged." The HUD flashed orange, and a graphic that looked like a loading screen appeared. Tiny bug-like bots emerged from an until-now-hidden slot in the WALYA's leg armor and began to scuttle around, fixing scrapes and tightening screws.

"Auto-repair? You amaze me, WALYA," I said.

"Just wait until you see my card tricks," the system replied. I managed a wheezing laugh, which hurt more than it should have. My ribs were bruised. Great.

Worse still was the fact that I had lost the high ground—and the drone was on the opposite side of the hill now. Things were looking dire. Maybe I could just make a break for the drone? No. The other exos were too fast. As soon as I turned my back, they'd strike. But I needed that comm module!

The WALYA finished the auto-repair, and I stood. Time to fight. I charged up the hill, fists balled and ready to swing—

—only to get knocked back out of the base by a joint attack. The two remaining teammates soared into the air above me, before dropping down with devastating kicks. I couldn't get around them! If I lowered my guard and tried to run, I'd be vulnerable to those blade wings. If I didn't run and just tried to fight my way through, time would run out before I even got close to the drone. And that was assuming I could even defeat them! There had to be some way. Think, Yared!

"Hostile analysis complete. Database match confirmed. Units designated Augur Hawk–class exoskeleton armor. Augur Hawk exo suits use antigravity webbing to glide for short distances. Highly mobile at middle speeds, but unable to maneuver in high-speed dives."

I perked up. "Reduced mobility, huh? WALYA, how much time is left in the match?"

"Two minutes, thirty seconds," the WALYA replied.

I grinned. "Perfect."

I charged up the hill again. That same sneering voice from the lead exo laughed in my ear. "Just give up, man! You and that suit both need to retire."

I was near the top when the two remaining suits shot out

of the base. They lifted into the air above me, gleaming like falling stars. Now that I knew what to look for, I could see the telltale sparkle of antigrav webbing on the underside of the exos' wings. They were like bigger, stronger, more dangerous versions of my nefasi at home. The two units swept down toward me, wing blades outstretched, ready to knock me out of the competition permanently.

But only if they could catch me.

I dropped the WALYA into a crouch.

"Ducking isn't going to help, loser!" the leader laughed again. He continued laughing right up until the point where I slammed the propulsion system on and shot up into the air, leaping right over the two hostiles.

"What the—"

"Sengis: PUNCH!" I shouted, slamming the WALYA's fist into the ground. A cloud of dust erupted, spreading quickly and reducing visibility. I sprang to my feet and dashed inside the base.

"You think that's funny?" the boy demanded. On my HUD, I saw his Augur Hawk zipping up the hill, followed by his teammate. I retreated to the opposite entrance.

"You never learn!" the boy laughed. "You can't block both entrances. Just hurry up and tap out."

Thirty seconds left.

"Hostiles incoming. Multiple attacks," the WALYA said.

The Augur Hawk leader flew through the northern entrance just as his teammate entered through the southern. Both of their blades were extended to their maximum range. "Game over, loser!" the leader shouted.

I grinned, then stepped backward. The two exos were unable to stop or dodge. The last thing I heard as they crashed into each other and tumbled to the floor was a wordless shout of rage. Music to my ears. I waved.

"Good game!" I called.

The air sparkled around me. "'Game over,'" I read as the timer reached zero. The drone! I ran outside and searched my HUD for its icon. There! It hadn't left the area yet but was slowly hovering in the air above the base. I sent the WALYA leaping into the air again and grabbed one of the drone's four rotor shields. The comm module was suspended beneath it by magnets. I sighed with relief and snagged it, dropping to the ground. It was the size of the WALYA's fist—dark gray and oval in shape. Gold prongs lined its underside, and a blinking strip of lights flashed red as I rotated it in my hands.

The module.

"Finally," I said. "Ready?"

"Indeed," said the WALYA. The armor in my left arm hissed open to reveal a hidden slot on its interior. There was a damaged comm module inside. I pried it out, grimacing as black char rubbed off. I slid the replacement into place, smiling when the light strip turned amber, then green, and a notification popped up on my HUD.

"Installation successful," the WALYA stated. "FTL communications operational. Unknown pilot interface, designated *Radial*, operational. Logging in with Radial system credentials. Welcome back, Yared. You have . . . two hundred thousand, seven hundred and fifty-one new messages."

I winced. No way was I going to listen to that many messages. Better to feign ignorance. Hopefully they'd be distracted by my sudden return. "Delete any from Uncle Moti, and send him my coordinates. Ask him to please send the Ibis to pick me up. Also, uh, tell them I'm okay."

"Deleting. You have . . . one new message. Priority status. It is not addressed to you, just to the holder of the comm module."

"Play it back." I frowned. Who would leave a message with anyone who could listen? People only did that in case of . . . emergencies. My eyes widened as the message crackled through my speakers.

"MAYDAY, MAYDAY, THIS IS THE INS *ADWA* AND WE'VE LOST CONTROL. I REPEAT, WE HAVE LOST

CONTROL AND ARE FALLING OUT OF ORBIT! YOU THERE, GET TO THE ESCAPE PODS, NOW! NOW! THAT'S AN ORDER!"

"But, sir—"

"GO, I'M RIGHT BEHIND YOU! MAYDAY! MAY— LOOK OUT!"

And the message went dead.

CHAPTER ELEVEN

"So let me get this straight," Uncle Moti said slowly over the ship's comm system. "The *Amba* wasn't attacked by pirates, but by . . . scrapper bots? And your Radial system accidentally activated a utility exoskeleton that hadn't been used in fifty years, which then rescued you and dropped you into the one location with an active game tournament? The one you've been begging to participate in for the last several months?"

I sat in the copilot's seat of a small Axumite scout ship, the INS *Menen*. The Ibis sat next to me, both hands on the controls and a look of concern on her face as she listened to me recap the last few hours. The WALYA was tucked in the tiny cargo area.

I had all sorts of medibots hovering around me, taking readings, shoving vitamin paste into my mouth, and just being overall worrywarts. Besa sat between me and the Ibis, squeezed in among the consoles and displays. Her head was on my knee, and I scratched behind her ears as I nodded.

"I know it sounds . . ." I trailed off as I tried to think of a word.

"Convenient?" Uncle Moti said.

"Foolish," the Ibis muttered. She pulled on the controls and sent the *Menen* farther up into the atmosphere, away from Old Earth.

"Mrowr."

I flicked Besa's ear. "Rude."

Uncle Moti scratched his beard from the display in front of us. Then he sighed. His face took up the main light-screen, and I could see new worry lines that I was pretty sure hadn't been there a few weeks ago. He looked at something off-screen that we couldn't see, pursed his lips, then sighed again.

"Leaving all that aside," he said. "I managed to have the emergency message traced. Had to pull a few strings and call in a few favors, but an old friend had some ancient equipment we managed to get working."

"Is everything okay there?" I asked anxiously.

He smiled. "New Amba has been through worse, my boy. It will hold."

"And Mom and Dad? Are they okay on the *Benevolence*? They weren't attacked, were they? Are they . . . ?"

I couldn't bring myself to say the words. Thankfully I didn't have to. Uncle Moti shook his head almost immediately. "They're fine. Itching to figure out who was behind the attack. Somebody put the scrappers up to it."

Scrappers were generally peaceful sentient AIs. According to Uncle Moti, a few Azmari-engineers studying the aftermath of the attack on the *Amba* discovered the bots had been reprogrammed. Nobody was saying any names, but I thought it had to be the pirates. What did Jemal call them? The Fallen.

"Your mother especially," Uncle Moti was saying. "I feel bad for the perpetrators if the Meshenitai ever let her join them in battle."

"I wish they could've come," I said, slumping back into my seat. Besa flicked her ears at me and lashed her tail, sharing in my distress.

"So do I," Uncle Moti said. "But they're needed elsewhere. And your ship, as fabulous as it is, couldn't fit everyone. Not if the Ibis was going to retrieve you. It barely fits Besa."

Besa growled, and everyone smiled.

Uncle Moti was right. With a narrow flight deck shaped like an egg and two knifelike wings on either side, the *Menen* was beautiful, dangerous, and very, very cramped. But hey, the pirates couldn't detect us, and as long as that was the case, I'd sing the *Menen*'s praises every day of the week—twice on Mondays.

"As I was saying," Uncle Moti continued, "we managed to isolate where the emergency message came from. I'm actually surprised you got an old maintenance exo to play it. I'll have to take a look at it when things are a bit calmer."

Uncle Moti's face disappeared and was replaced by a star chart with several blinking coordinates in the middle. "Recognize this area?" he asked.

I squinted. "Sort of . . ."

"That's Debris Town," the Ibis said, shocked. "Above Old Earth. Why would an emergency message be coming from there?"

"I don't know," Uncle Moti said grimly. "I would like to know how the comm module ended up on Old Earth. I don't know if the message was recorded before it was scavenged and traveled in the hold of some junk freighter to Debris Town, or after. Either way, and as much as I hate and will regret saying this, we need to investigate. This is our only clue to Adwa. It might be our shot at discovering its whereabouts. Maybe our only shot."

"Don't worry, Uncle Moti," I said, "we're going to get to the bottom of this, right?" I looked at the Ibis, who put on a brave face and nodded. Besa yawned like she had nothing better to do.

"I have to hope so," Uncle Moti said. "I have to."

The Ibis and I argued for half an hour over the best way to

sneak into Debris Town. It was like a small asteroid belt—a pirates' haven! There would be all sorts of deserted ships and junk and space trash, but also homes and people just trying to live. There might even be automated defenses trying to protect turf and stolen goods and . . . and . . . whatever else pirates considered valuable.

Just to be safe, we gave the ship a fake name and transponder code, which the Ibis explained was like an ID badge for vessels. It let other ships and space stations know who we were. Probably not the best idea when trying to break into a pirates' lair.

But in the end, entering was as simple as flying in. The Ibis pulled into an empty berth set inside the desolate hangar bay of an old luxury yacht. The place was guarded by only a rusty automated sentry drone, its power reserves blinking red.

"This . . . seems too simple," I whispered as we crept past the drone. We snuck into a dusty alcove and pulled up the map Uncle Moti had transmitted to us. In this section of Debris Town, someone had rigged together several abandoned ships into a sort of space apartment complex. There was only the one entrance, so we had to be careful.

"Don't complain when the orbital farm produces more," the Ibis said. Her attention was on the cube-shaped map that she twisted and expanded between her hands.

"What?"

"It's a saying my mom would always tell us when we started questioning our good fortune. Basically, be quiet and be thankful before you jinx us."

I zipped my lips and threw away the imaginary key. Besa, panicking, thought I'd actually thrown something away and nearly bounded off trying to find it. Only my death grip on her tail stopped her from rushing out into full view of anyone passing by.

"This is like babysitting two firecrackers that keep hurling themselves into the fire," the Ibis muttered. Suddenly she stiffened, then rapidly pulled her hands apart to blow the map up to twenty times its original size. She stabbed a finger at a blinking silver dot, inside of what appeared to be half a wrecked colony ship.

"There," she said. "That's where we need to go—the *Hope*. An old colony ship that was meant to travel to a habitable planet a couple solar systems over, before Adwa was lost and no one could use the navigation system. It's been floating in orbit ever since, picked apart for scraps. According to your uncle, that's where the emergency request was recorded."

I gawked at the size of the colony ship. "We're supposed to just walk over there, through hundreds of pirates? After which we'll . . . what . . . ? Ask everyone nearby about a piece of priceless ancient technology?"

"Not we," the Ibis said, smiling sweetly. "*You*. The fewer the better. I'm going to stay here on the *Menen* and keep an eye on what's happening. Its sensors are better than anything within a thousand miles. You take your . . . exo. And Besa, who will be in stealth mode. Trust me, you'll fit right in with the trash."

I wanted to argue just on principle, but after taking a moment to think about it, I knew she was right. "Fine. Come on, Besa. Someone around here has to do some real work."

At first glance, Debris Town was a junk-filled asteroid field. Something you avoided rather than used as a hiding place, let alone made it your home. And the number of scavenged ships! Skeletal frames filled the space: battle cruisers, scout ships, cargo shuttles, tiny message couriers, giant automated repair freighters . . . I even saw a couple power armor carriers! They were huge hive-like vessels, their exo pods dark and empty and their hulls pitted and cratered.

It was a space graveyard. Broken ships with their hulls ripped to shreds and their insides floating next to their outsides. Asteroids ranging in size from marbles to spaceports.

There was even a semi-functional satellite that went hurtling through space, on a mission that only it remembered.

It just felt . . . empty.

But then I started to see signs of life. Of organization. Cables were everywhere, at first invisible against the dark of space. But every now and then I'd see something resembling a spiderweb stretching between what I once thought was chaos. Lines connected one half of a shuttle with another, the life-support systems in both still active. More connected a trio of shipping containers the size of a kebele bus to a cargo ship with a functional engine. It was still glowing, still powered up. That cargo ship wasn't carrying anything big anytime soon, but someone was living inside of it. And apparently they were part of a community.

A *pirate* community, I reminded myself. I had to be vigilant. Drifting through space with nothing but an old exo to protect me was scary.

But not as scary as the ghosts.

"Movement detected, thirty meters ahead."

WHAM!

The WALYA's voice startled me, and I jumped in my harness, slamming my head into the top of my helmet.

"Who is it?" I asked, grimacing in pain. The system didn't answer. "WALYA, highlight the targets."

"No targets detected," the AI answered.

"What? You just said—"

"Movement detected!" the speakers blared. A red light winked on my HUD before disappearing just as quickly. What was going on?

The Ibis sounded skeptical when I mentioned it to her. "What are you talking about?"

I was gently navigating around a booster rocket someone had attached to a solar collection sail. I let the WALYA do most of the piloting while I monitored the heads-up display. Besa floated beside me, her ears pressed flat against her diranium skull. She may have gotten all the upgrades for Guardian EVAs, but she still wasn't happy about using them to float around in space.

"I can't really explain it," I said. "It's like I get a brief warning, a flashing red alert, and then it disappears."

"It can't disappear. That doesn't happen."

"Yes, I know it's not supposed to happen but—look, it's doing it again!" A brief flurry of red dots burst along the top of my HUD, then disappeared, like fireworks during Enkutatash. "Are you seeing anything on the *Menen*'s sensors?"

The Ibis didn't answer for several seconds. When she did, she sounded concerned. "Yared, everything is fine over here. Maybe . . . maybe it's the WALYA? You did say it was old. Its sensors could be degraded."

"Maybe," I said reluctantly. I didn't know why, but I was hesitant to blame the sensor ghosts on the exo. Call me sentimental (it's one of my nicknames), but the WALYA had saved my life twice now. It had helped me win against a trio of overpowered players at the Royal Trials. I was starting to think that just because it was old didn't mean it was useless.

Wow, I really channeled Uncle Moti with that thought. Ugh. Next thing you know, I'd be laughing super hard and talking at the top of my voice on a holocall with friends while we compare vintage breath mints. Horrifying.

Besa and I floated through the long cabin of a luxury yacht someone had converted into a tiny orbital farm. It was impressive actually—they'd rigged the zero-gravity sauna to grow coffee, jasmine, and other useful crops. Without gravity to hold them down, the plants grew in spiraling balls of different colors and sizes, until the room looked like a solar system of plants. Pretty amazing, right?

I was still marveling at the ingenious creativity when we exited the yacht and floated to a stop.

"Um," I said.

"What is it?" the Ibis immediately responded. "You should be right on top of the ship. Can you see it?"

"Um."

"Stop saying um! Yes or no? Can you see it? Is your sensor acting up again? Is the ship there?"

"Yes," I said, glancing at Besa. "And no."

As an annoyed Ibis muttered horrendous threats that no pure soul such as me should ever have to hear, the two of us gawked at the sight in front of us.

The forgotten colony ship was in fact there. Shaped like one of those long balloons Uncle Moti would sell part-time at Enkutatash, it stretched out so far that I couldn't see the back half. The thing was so wide it had to have its own orbit. Rings separated the massive vessel into sections. If I zoomed in the display on my HUD far enough, I could just make out writing on the hull.

"Colony Ship 002," I said out loud. "The *Hope*. Looks like it never even finished construction."

"Mrowr."

"Yeah," I said. "I guess it never will."

The Ibis sounded annoyed as her voice came through my speakers. "What are you talking about?"

"They're tearing it apart," I said softly.

Four huge crane-like arms emerged from a gaping gash in the ship, like a giant spider emerging from the skeleton of some mysterious space behemoth. Each arm ended in three hook claws that were currently peeling back the hull of the colony ship like the rind of a fruit. Wreckage and debris floated out into space—accompanied by tiny dots of light floating this way and that. When I zoomed in, I realized they were smaller ships harvesting useful parts.

"Who's tearing it apart?" the Ibis asked. "I'm not seeing anything on the *Menen*'s sensors."

I frowned. "Something's wrong with the WALYA's screen as well. The HUD is . . . well, it's going wild."

The WALYA's screen suddenly went black. I couldn't see anything. "Stealth transmitter detected nearby," the WALYA said. "Rebooting targeting and sensor modules and recalibrating. Ten seconds until reboot complete."

"Yared, what's going on?" the Ibis asked. "You disappeared off my screen."

"I don't know!" I shouted.

She inhaled. "Oh no. I count . . . four unknown targets heading your way. I don't know where they came from. They just appeared out of nowhere!"

The HUD winked back on. "The sensor platform on the INS *Menen* has been updated as well to counteract stealth technology."

"You can do that?" I asked.

"It can do that?" the Ibis repeated.

"Mrowr?"

I swear I could hear a hint of smugness in the WALYA's

response. "It would be surprising if I could not. I will inform you of my functionality since interfacing with your Radial system—which is also detailed in the manual I provided for you—"

"Yared the Gr8 doesn't do manuals," the Ibis and I said at the same time.

"—but that will have to come at a later date, as there are four hostile exos approaching your position. Scans indicate a new combat profile. Designation: Golden Wolf."

Four Golden Wolves? That was practically a whole squadron of . . . whatever those exos were! Had the pirates finally noticed our arrival? Maybe the best thing for us to do would be to turn around and link back up with the *Menen*. We could outrun them and hightail it back to the *Amba*. Yeah, that's what we would—

Four gold-and-silver exos appeared on my HUD. I zoomed in and groaned. They were heavily armored and much bigger than the WALYA. Huge rocket thrusters mounted on each limb allowed them to maneuver incredibly well through space. Each carried an energy scythe with not one, but two curved, flickering blades the color of sunset.

When the leader twirled their weapon and extended it to point at me, the blades looked like fangs snapping in the night.

Golden wolves, indeed.

"Okay, time to retreat, WALYA," I said.

The sound of somebody choking echoed through my helmet speakers. "Did you just say . . . retreat?" the Ibis asked.

"Yes. Prep the *Menen*; we're getting out of here."

"You. Yared the Gr8. Retreating?"

I rolled my eyes. "Yes, believe it or not. This is too big a fight for us right now. Maybe we can sneak back and search for the origin of the emergency broadcast later."

"Okaaaay," the Ibis said. "I'm just saying, you're the one who refused to skate backward in the holorink because, and I quote, 'Yared the Gr8 doesn't back away from anything.' And then you busted your head because—"

"Okay!" I said loudly. "I get it. WALYA, I think it's time to try out the Augur Hawk combat profile. The one you copied during the Royal Trials."

"Ready on your command," the system said.

I flicked open the Radial (wow, it felt good to have that technology available again) and selected the new spread-winged profile of the Augur Hawk on my left wrist. Then I chose the diving bird of prey image on my right wrist. "Augur Hawk: Piercing Sky mode."

The WALYA vibrated for a split second. The armor on the exo's shoulders lifted, revealing a previously unseen opening. A bright, blinding flash of light exploded out as a giant pair of electric-blue energy wings emerged from the exo. I could feel them humming through the armor. It was incredible!

"All right," I said. "We're heading back to the *Menen*. These pirates aren't getting anything except a face full of space dust. Ready? Here we—"

"I know you."

A strange voice came through the secure channel of my comm system. I frowned. How had they gotten access? This was supposed to be Axum only!

"Selam, Axum," the voice said again. "Stars of the saints . . . is it really you?"

I froze.

The Golden Wolves had come to an abrupt stop. The leader sheathed their energy scythe and extended both arms of the exo. An icon popped up on-screen. An elderly woman stared at me with an expression somewhere between sorrow and overwhelming joy. She smiled as a tear ran down her face, and as she spoke, more icons popped up on-screen. Dozens. Hundreds! They began to appear on top of one another as the HUD became more and more crowded. All of them had the same location signature: the *Hope*. But at the center was the leader, who raised her hand in a salute even as her exo did the same.

"It *is* you! Stars be praised. Young Yared, prince of kings. You don't recognize me, do you? How could you? You were a baby when Moti took you."

"I'm sorry," I said, still a bit on edge. "Who are you?"

She laughed. "Ah, Moti, always teaching caution. My name, sweet boy, is Yasmiin Berihun." She laughed again, this time at my incredulous expression as the name registered. "Exactly. And I will have my stubborn, bullheaded, tej-drinking goat of a husband cleaning the gunk out of my thrusters for a year if he never mentioned your aunt Yas."

CHAPTER TWELVE

"I know you," I said suddenly.

The conversation died around me. We were all standing in an elevator that climbed the exterior of the dismantled colony ship—me, the Ibis, and a very fussy Besa. (Who knew the bionic lioness preferred not to float in the black void of space for extended periods of time?)

And Aunt Yas.

The Golden Wolves and the WALYA were at the docks getting much-needed tune-ups. The Ibis had docked the *Menen* as soon as I called.

"I would hope so," Aunt Yas said with a wink. "We exchanged introductions only a few minutes ago."

"No," I said, trying and failing to keep a smile off my face. "I know *that*. It's just . . ."

"Can you go five minutes without being weird?" the Ibis asked. Her face was pressed against the thick plastiglass as she stared at the activity going on around the ship.

I ignored her. Besa nudged my hip with her head, and I

scratched her ears absentmindedly. There was a feeling of familiarity when I looked at Aunt Yas. Almost like . . .

"Summer skies," I sang softly. "Soaring on freedom's wings."

Aunt Yas stiffened, while the Ibis and Besa both looked at me as if I'd suddenly grown two extra heads. (Which, to be honest, would've helped with the harmony.)

"Evening moon," Aunt Yas whisper-sang. "Light the path to guide them home."

"Until the day we next meet," we sang together, "children from the stars, be strong."

Aunt Yas broke off and wiped a tear that trailed down her face. She sniffed, then laughed and shook her head. "I haven't heard that in nearly a decade. Excuse my tears, children—and lioness," she added.

"Uncle Moti would sing that all the time," I said. "Well . . . nowadays he just hums the tune. But I saw a vid of him once, singing with a woman in a duet. That was you, wasn't it?"

She smiled. "It's a lullaby we sing to newborn children on Axum. Moti and I used to sing it to you all the time."

I didn't have a chance to ask any more questions, because at that moment, the elevator slowed to a stop and the circular doors spiraled open. "We're here," Aunt Yas said, and stepped out. After a shared look, the Ibis and I followed, Besa by my side.

We stepped through a thin corridor onto the topmost deck of the colony ship, as wide as the People's Chamber back on Harar Station, where the Azmari performed for my parents. And it was just as beautiful—at least, it used to be.

The floor rose and fell in looping patterns. It took me a few seconds to realize it was designed that way to create natural benches for people to sit. The walls curved up to the ceiling and were covered in plants. Herbs, flowers, even a few edible vegetables—they'd grown wild. Vines snaked across the walkway, entangling around the few remaining hovering light fixtures. It smelled like a garden. If not for the giant gash that severed the viewing gallery in half—sealed from space by only an energy barrier—I thought it would've been absolutely perfect.

But, I mean, there was that giant gash.

"This was the Reflection Deck," Aunt Yas said softly. "It was intended to allow the families who would be traveling on the *Hope* to garden, meditate, and make peace with leaving Old Earth to build a new and better life among the stars."

"The *Hope*," I repeated.

She nodded, but it was the Ibis who spoke next. "It was

going to carry an entire community of botanists and farmers," she said. "Most of them were family and extended family. They were headed to a nearby star system and would have provided food and medical help for the people there . . . but it never launched. Without Adwa, it was impossible."

"And now it's destroyed," I said, staring at the destruction. "Was this done by the pirates, too?"

Aunt Yas turned around, confused. "What pirates?"

I frowned. "The pirates who've been terrorizing Old Earth and New Amba, and then hiding in Debris Town. The Fallen. You haven't seen them? Balamba Ras seemed pretty upset with them. They destroyed a comms array and sent scrappers to attack New Amba just a few days ago."

Aunt Yas shook her head slowly. "That's impossible."

"But we saw the newsvids," the Ibis said. She pulled up her wrist comm and tapped in a command. A video appeared above her arm, and she scrubbed the timeline forward.

We all watched the mysterious battle cruiser appear out of the stars and fire missiles at different targets around Old Earth before zooming off, and then the video was over. The Ibis played it again, slowing it down and zooming in as Aunt Yas knelt for a closer look.

Finally, Aunt Yas straightened, playing with the graying locs draped over her shoulder.

"I've never seen any ship of that sort in all the years I've been here," Aunt Yas said.

"Mrowr."

I nodded thoughtfully. "Good point, Besa. Could they be hiding from you somewhere in Debris Town? In all the junk floating around?"

"No. Absolutely not. My Golden Wolves patrol the area regularly. We can go where ships cannot. Besides, there's no way anyone could hide something of that size. The energy signature would give it away immediately. No, if this happened, that ship came from somewhere else. And I have suspicions where."

Silence fell. I tried to fit this new information into the growing puzzle of Adwa. Everyone had been so positive that Debris Town was where the pirates came from, where they made their base. But now Aunt Yas said that was impossible. It was all one big tangled mess, and lives were on the line. Would we never reunite our home?

A notification dinged, and Aunt Yas popped open a message window above her wrist comm. "Yes?"

"Sensor reports from the last sweep are in."

She glanced at us. "I'll be right there. I want to check something out." She closed the window and pointed us to one of the few functional areas on the Reflection Deck. "You all stay here. I'm going to look at our last sweep data and verify that we don't have any extra visitors sneaking around. All this talk about pirates is making me jumpy."

She turned to leave, then paused and glanced back at me. At the woman's look, the Ibis suddenly patted Besa on her flank and nodded to a cluster of workstations. "Come on, Besa. Let's make sure you didn't damage anything floating through space like you have no sense."

The two walked away, and Aunt Yas smiled after them. "I'm glad you were able to make some friends, Yared. We . . . I was worried."

"Yeah," I said. "They're great. I just wish . . . well . . ."

"What?"

I shrugged. "Everyone is doing their own thing these days. The Ibis is doing astrogation training for the Meshenitai, and Besa is taking on new Guardian duties. And me . . . I'm just sitting and doing nothing while my friends are all being great. It feels weird."

"Hmm, I guess I can see that. But friendships don't have a distance limit on them. I think you'll find that though you may be separated, might even go years without seeing each other, the next time you're together it will be as if no time had passed at all."

I looked up at her. For a moment, it felt like she wasn't talking about me. "Is that how it is for you and Uncle Moti?"

She nodded with a soft, sad smile. "I hope so. We were supposed to meet as soon as Moti reached the system, but . . . well, he was delayed. Now I see why. Sometimes life throws a grav wrench into your plans . . . You just have to build around it. Strong relationships, like the ones you have with your friends over there, they'll grow around whatever issues there might be."

We reached the elevator, and Aunt Yas leaned against the wall as she waited for the doors to open. "How is he?" she asked without looking at me.

I grinned. "Still burning his sambusas."

A bright peal of laughter slipped out of Aunt Yas's mouth. She covered it with both hands as her shoulders shook. The elevator spiraled open, and she stepped inside, still laughing.

"That's my husband," she said. "Now—stay here. I'll be back shortly, and we will figure out what to do next."

I sighed. Why was that the only thing people wanted me to do? Waiting is hard! Maybe I should change my Nexus ID from Yared the Gr8 to Yared Sit-and-Wait. Taking out enemies with the incredible weapon of patience.

"Yared!" The Ibis's shout interrupted my misery party before I could really lay it on thick. Shame. I had a few good lines I hadn't used yet.

"What's up?" I asked, jogging over.

"We've got a problem. Show him, Besa."

The lioness stood and placed a metal paw on the workstation. A blank vidscreen materialized.

I frowned. "Besa, are you a hacker now?"

The Ibis shushed me. "Just watch, boy! We can finally see the video part of that message on your comm module! Look who sent it!"

A thin, hawk-faced man I'd never seen before appeared on the vidscreen, with a mustache that made the giant custodian-bot sweepers look like kids' toys. He appeared exhausted, and when he rubbed his eyes, one hand was heavily bandaged.

"Mayday, Mayday, this is the INS *Adwa*, and we've lost control. I repeat, we have lost control and are falling out of orbit. You there, get to the escape pods, now! Now! That's an order!"

"But, sir—"

"Go, I'm right behind you! Mayday! May— Look out!"

The voice stopped. I pounded my fist on the workstation. "It's the same message! We're right back where we—" The Ibis gripped my wrist. Besa's tail lashed furiously just as I stopped short and gawked at the screen.

The man had turned and stepped back from the screen, gesturing at something to his crew off camera. All around him, people sprinted toward the escape pods. And that's when I realized that the man had no intention of following them. He was going to stay with the ship. Was that the captain? The video cut off soon after, but just before it did, for a split second, the strange man pulled something with his good hand and fitted it to his face. Something I recognized immediately.

A silver-and-black mask—the same kind worn by Mesfina.

CHAPTER THIRTEEN

"That's impossible," I said, still staring at the frozen image on the vidscreen. The injured man wearing Mesfina's mask was looking back over his shoulder as he recorded his call for help. I clenched my fists at the silver-and-black mask with Axum's symbol etched on the side.

But the Ibis shook her head. "That's what I said. And yet . . ." She gestured at the vidscreen.

"So . . . Mesfina—the one back on New Amba—escaped Adwa but doesn't know where it crashed? He left this message? I mean, why would he do that? What's the reason? Or . . ."

My voice trailed off, but the Ibis continued the sentence for me. "Or the person we met isn't really Mesfina."

An impostor? Why? Why go through all that trouble to impersonate someone . . . for over ten years!

My eyes flicked to the vidscreen and landed on the—I forced myself to say it—the real Mesfina's eyes. He was looking right back at me. A trinket dangled from his neck, and I swear I'd seen it before. But it was his gaze I couldn't tear away from. He looked straight into the camera, even as he pointed at the controls, like he was telling everyone he would stay with Adwa and go down with it. That was weird. In fact . . .

"Why record this?" I mumbled aloud.

"What?" The Ibis looked at me strangely. "It's a distress signal. They were being attacked."

"No, sorry, you're right about that. But . . . why record video, when just the audio was enough? Audio would have resulted in a smaller file size that could be sent anywhere. It wouldn't have to be stored on a comm module that could . . ."

I stopped. Stared at the screen.

"Yared?"

"Mrowr."

I squinted and leaned into the screen. "Can I see something, Besa? Zoom in. Right there. Yeah." I pointed at the vidscreen and glanced at the Ibis. "That message was sent on a comm module that can only be powered by an Axumite exo unit and could only be viewed using Axumite technology. He wanted to make sure the message fell into the right hands."

"Who? Him?" The Ibis pointed at the real Mesfina.

I nodded. "Yep. Because whoever received it had the key to finding Adwa."

"So it's nearby? We need to tell your uncle! Maybe get a message to him somehow—we can take the *Menen* and slip through the rubble field again. Get search parties." The Ibis started to rise, but I placed a hand on her shoulder and shook my head.

"No."

"What?" she asked. "Why not? Yared, we're so close to finding Adwa. You can't get scared now."

I grinned. "Scared? No, you don't understand. We don't need to do all of that because I already know where Adwa is."

She stared at me. Besa actually growled in disbelief. I patted her flank and nodded at the screen, where the real Mesfina was pointing at the controls.

"Look. He's got the destination programmed into the flight controls. That's why there was video with the message. When you listen to just the audio, it sounds like there's silence. It's additional security."

The Ibis was already tapping the coordinates from the vidscreen into her wrist comm, mumbling as she calculated trajectories on the fly. She was really going to be an incredible astrogator.

"Got it," she said after a few seconds. "Besa, I need your help."

The lioness padded over, and a holokeyboard appeared on her side. The Ibis entered in her calculations, and Besa stretched her mouth open wide, as if she were yawning. Light flickered out as she projected a star chart in the space between us.

"If this is us," the Ibis murmured, "and this is the point where the Mayday was issued, those coordinates would take us . . . here." She jabbed a finger at the star chart, and we both leaned in to see.

"Wait, I know that place." I gripped the edge of the workstation in surprise.

"You do?"

I nodded. "That's where—"

My Radial pulsed, and the wrist comm the Ibis wore chimed. Besa snapped her mouth shut. The star chart disappeared as she roared in alarm. High above in the vidscreens on the ceiling, light bloomed in a sudden flare. I thought it was an error with the screens at first, until I realized the workstation monitor was showing the same thing. *Something is wrong*, I thought just as Aunt Yas's face materialized in a vid-alert.

"Children! Get to your ship!" Her face was calm, but her voice was frantic.

"What's wrong?" I asked.

She scowled. "That battle cruiser you asked about? It just blasted its way through the rubble field surrounding Debris Town."

*   *   *

The Golden Wolves were already in the sky by the time we'd reached the docking bay. It had been a struggle fighting our way through the *Hope*. Everybody on the colony ship wanted to be somewhere else, either fleeing like we were or hunkering down to take shelter and try to outlast whatever was on the horizon.

There was an unfortunate sort of beauty to the chaos. Families pooled supplies, the adults building barricades and the children handing out emergency rations. An older sister strapped on her younger sister's EVA helmet before dealing with her own. An old man passed around water bulbs from floating crates in front of his restaurant. Terrible, horrible moments of tenderness.

"It's like they've been through this before," I said as we hurried aboard the *Menen*. The WALYA was locked into position on the underside of the ship. The Ibis quickly got us flight ready as I secured Besa. Didn't want a half-ton Guardian rattling around puncturing holes in the ship.

"Because they have," Aunt Yas's voice said. She popped up on the main screen in a separate window as sensor footage of the battle cruiser filled the screen. "So many times before. There aren't any pirates in Debris Town, Yared, but there are survivors of pirate-like behavior. You want to see a pirate? Try to leave Debris Town in search of a better, more stable life. Moti used to say you could build a spaceship with all the red tape." She shook her head, as if to rid herself of the negative thoughts.

Something in her words sounded familiar. Hadn't Jemal mentioned something similar? He'd said the pirates, the Fallen, just wanted access to the IU for better opportunities. Had he been talking about Debris Town? And why would he call them pirates?

"Now," Aunt Yas continued, "you all have to leave. Enough chatter. Get clear of Debris Town and use the *Hope* for cover. Once you're out, you head straight to Moti and don't look back, you hear me? Don't look back."

"What about you?" I shouted before she could break the link. "Don't you want to see Uncle Moti? Come with us!"

She smiled that same soft, sad smile she had when talking about her husband. About my uncle. "Moti and I made a promise a long time ago. He took you and protected you, and I can't abandon our people on the *Hope*, either. Not when they need me most. We've all sacrificed too much to stop right at the end."

I remembered Uncle Moti talking to me about sacrifices back on the kebele bus. Now, finally, I think it all clicked. He and Aunt Yas had given up so much to make sure Axum could return for its people. It was their shared love of their home and its freedom that was only made stronger by their love for each other.

"When all of Axum is reunited," I said softly.

Aunt Yas smiled and nodded. "When all of Axum is reunited. Now go."

The feed cut out, and I slammed my fist into the arm of my chair. The *Menen*'s docking restraints released and the Ibis began to speed toward the far side of the *Hope*. On the main screen, four Golden Wolves raced in the opposite direction. I didn't know what Aunt Yas's plan was for the battle cruiser, but I did know that four tiny exos weren't going to stop it for long.

The WALYA's cute, cartoony goat icon appeared on-screen, its charming image at complete odds with the message it delivered.

"Yasmiin Berihun installed an upgrade for my systems while you were away, with instructions not to open it until you were safely away."

"What is it?" I asked, my eyes focused on the exos.

"It appears to be a new combat profile, designated Golden Wolf."

The hull of the *Hope* came on-screen, blocking the looming confrontation from the *Menen*. I balled my fists tight and looked at the Ibis.

She sighed. "I take it we're not going to go find your uncle like she said?"

"Since when have adults ever known what's good for them?" I asked.

"True," she said.

"Mrowr," Besa agreed.

"Mature human caretakers have been known to make mistakes," the WALYA said. "Your statement, though phrased as a question, is factual."

"Glad we all agree," I said. "We're going to Adwa."

"This isn't Adwa," the Ibis said. She groaned as she spun around in her chair to face me, an accusatory expression on her face. "I know you did not do what I think you just did."

"Mrowr," Besa yowled from her harness. If she wasn't restrained, I'd probably be pinned under two sets of diranium claws.

The WALYA did the AI version of sucking its teeth as it spoke, which turned out to be a burst of static coming through the speakers. "You have set back human-AI relationships by another millennium with your actions." The armored suit had disengaged from the *Menen* and was in self-pilot mode, standing outside the ship like someone's angry parent picking up their child late from school.

I beamed. "What, none of you have faith in me? In Yared the Gr8? Why not?"

Three glares (one of them a holomoji goat) were aimed in my direction. I shook my head and unfastened my restraints. "Oh, ye of little faith," I said, stepping to the *Menen*'s hatch and hitting the release button. "One day you will learn."

The hatch spiraled open to reveal the gloomy and overgrown Gibe Arena. The Ibis had landed on the same platform where I first encountered Nefasati. I shuddered at the memory, then brushed it aside. I had more important things to do at the moment. The scrappers were already rebuilding their assembly hive towers—more of them than before—and I could see many of the bots scurrying around the shadows below us. Even without Nefasati's stalking presence, they were expanding the nest. Good. I searched the northwest corner for what I needed to make my plan work, then grinned when I found it. Perfect.

"Why are you smirking?" the Ibis asked. "You do realize the coordinates brought us to the wrong place, right? An old games arena. This doesn't look like Adwa at all. Wonderful. And this is—conveniently, I might add—really close to where you were playing in the Royal Trials *without me and Besa*. Don't think we forgot. When this is all over, you owe us."

"Of course," I said, spreading my arms wide. "You're absolutely right. The old me would've mentioned that playing in that game was for the greater Axum good. The new and improved Yared the Gr8 won't mention that at all because he is a selfless and humble kid. Gracious. Kind. Meek, even—hey, Besa, why aren't you recording this speech? I want to watch it later."

The Ibis groaned, and Besa growled something so rude my ears started burning. I rolled my eyes.

"I was just kidding, jeez. Anyway, I don't think there were any games played here at all."

"Mrowr?"

I patted Besa's flank, careful to avoid her spikes. "Yes, I know it's called the Gibe Arena, but it wasn't an arena for games—which . . . seems like a cruel oversight. It was an arena for performances, like the Azmari who sang on Harar Station."

The Ibis frowned. "So you think the Gibe Arena is near Adwa?

"Nope. The arena is a *part* of Adwa. We're standing on top of it right now!"

The Ibis, Besa, and the WALYA looked at me, then peered over the edge of the platform (which was actually a stage), then looked at one another.

"He's finally lost it," the Ibis mumbled.

"Human children often go wayward in their search for societal approval." The WALYA folded its arms and shook its helmet. "Such a shame."

I sighed. Geniuses were often unappreciated by their peers. They would have to be shown.

"Fine," I said. "I'll show you."

And I jumped over the edge.

"Yared!" the Ibis shouted, but my birhani was already out. I raced down the steep arena walls, avoiding crumbling seats and the occasional napping scrapper. Without Nefasati or the pirates to rile them up, they were actually pretty cool. Like robotic bumblebees the size of dogs who just wanted to dig day in and day out.

And I knew the reason why.

I reached the dim floor and swerved around scrapper towers. A few of the locust drones fluttered about the tops, but they ignored me. The birhani cast a soft amber glow over everything as I hummed along, revealing intricate patterns on the floor that narrowed into tight, geometric shapes around the base of the assembly hives. I slowed, looking for something in particular. If I remembered correctly, it was right around . . . there!

"Yared, wait up!

The Ibis's voice sounded from somewhere in the distance. I stepped off the birhani and raised it high in the air, waving it like a spotlight for the others to find. Soon, Besa, the WALYA, and the Ibis appeared out of the dark, murderous expressions on everyone's faces.

"Before you attack," I said, cutting off a growl from Besa, "Ibis, what's your least-favorite chore?"

"Babysitting you," she said, folding her arms.

"Point taken. Second-least-favorite chore. One that you always try to trade with someone to get out of doing."

She flung her arm back in the direction we came. "Clearing out those creepy nests! You know that. Which is why you owe me big-time when we get back. This is beyond creepy—it's disgusting, so hurry up!"

I let a fierce grin cross my face. "And why do we have to clear them out?"

This time the WALYA answered, and if an AI could sound reflective, it certainly did. "Scrappers, as you call them, cluster around signal emitters and use the radiation waves as an energy source to replicate."

The Ibis's eyes widened, and she punched me in the shoulder. Seriously, why was that her response to getting excited? I'd hate to be around her on her birthday. No one would escape unharmed. "Communication centers. They build their nest around communication centers!"

"Yep," I said proudly. "And we just so happen to be looking for an enormous astrolabe, aka a giant, oversized communication device." I lifted the birhani so the light landed on an odd-looking assembly hive extending high out of the arena floor, scrapper cables zigzagging in and out of it.

"WALYA, Sengis Punch."

The exo took two steps forward, leapt high in the air, then dropped on top of the hive with a ferocious ground punch. We all stepped back several paces as the hive exploded into a cloud of circuitry and cables.

A hatchway stood beneath it. Black metal, no rust in sight, and with a Ge'ez placard fastened above it.

"'Operations,'" I read, then stepped forward and activated my Radial. "Lij Yared of Axum."

More Ge'ez appeared in a silvery flourish in the air in front of the door. *Welcome to Adwa Strategic Command Mobile Operations, Lij Yared.*

The hatch spiraled open, and I bowed, gesturing the others to drop down ahead of me. "Welcome to Adwa."

CHAPTER FOURTEEN

We descended into an unlit corridor with only the glow from my birhani to light our way. I kept my Radial active as well, just in case. The WALYA couldn't fit through the hatchway, so it was keeping an eye out for any nosy scrappers trying to seal us inside. The exo also kept up a steady stream of commentary, using the sensor link from the Radial to keep tabs on what was going on. It made me feel just a little bit better hearing it talk. Sort of.

"It's not like an adaptive power armor suit built using Axumite technology could've benefited from visiting the interior of the facility. Typical human oversight to build substandard entryways that prevent synthetics from entering."

"Didn't AIs help build Adwa as well?" the Ibis asked.

Have you ever heard an AI sniff in annoyance? It sounds like static. "Well, humans designed its blueprints. So . . . Oh, hello, tiny one. Terribly sorry, I can't let you do that. Scans show there is a lovely bloom of radiation rising from a crack in the floor about ten meters that way. Would you like to build a hive there? Yes? Excellent. Please let me know if you require assistance."

I stopped, confused. "WALYA, who are you talking to?"

The kindness dropped from its voice as it responded. "A scrapper bot. It wanted to build over the hatchway."

"You're never that nice to me."

"What was that? I can always seal you in myself."

Besa growled, and the WALYA immediately sounded contrite. "Of course *you* would be allowed to exit. You are a force of good."

The Ibis snorted, then stopped. I immediately lifted the birhani higher, trying to crane my neck and see what had spooked her. "What is it?"

"You hear that?" She cocked her head. "Or rather, feel that?"

"I don't—" I broke off because I did actually feel something. A vibration similar to a large piece of running equipment. It felt sort of like the metal extractor Uncle Moti used to keep in the warehouse back on Addis Prime, the one he'd feed junk and take the excess material to sell. But that was a faint sensation compared with the one I felt now. When I focused on it, I could feel my teeth chatter.

We squeezed our way through the final length of the corridor, navigating through partially collapsed walls and a pile of what looked suspiciously like a scrapper had eaten something that disagreed with it. Did scrappers eat or did they just . . . absorb radiation? On second thought, I didn't want to examine a scrapper's digestive tendencies too closely. A final hatchway waited at the end of the tunnel, and when I stepped forward, it spiraled open. We walked through—

—and froze.

"Is that . . . ?" I began.

"Mrowr?" Besa asked.

"Hnnngggg," the Ibis grunted, either in pure joy or incredulous disbelief.

"Apologies, but is everyone functioning at what humans consider adequate levels?" the WALYA asked, its voice filtering through our wrist comms. "Because sensors indicate you . . . are not."

I shook my head, tried to speak, then shook my head again. It was just so . . . incredible.

It was obvious Adwa was a continuation of Harar Station, even if I hadn't seen a diagram of the Axum capital throne ship. This place was big beyond measure. Like, how do you measure an ocean? Or space? (Don't answer that. I know there are actual technical measurements, but imagine seeing them for the first time and trying to describe what you were looking at. Yeah. I thought so.)

Harar Station was definitely larger, but it was divided in modules and quarters and residences and atriums. This was just . . . space. Four metallic-gray walls that were so big I thought my eyes would roll to the back of my head if they kept looking up. They were covered in long ridges that took me forever to realize were workstations for personnel. The walls tapered inward at the top, so the rectangular ceiling was smaller than the floor.

High above, an oval structure was slowly descending toward us. Our arrival had triggered a response.

That was the second-most-important thing in the room.

The first was the ginormous holodisplay of an astrolabe floating inside of a cube of light. And when I say ginormous, I mean it was easily the size of the Gebeya, Axum's secret-FTL-drive-disguised-as-a-marketplace, back before Axum reappeared in Addis Prime.

The astrolabe's three data loops swirled gently around it in opposing directions. Lines of calculations streamed from the center. Really! I could actually see mathematical equations and astrogation projections fizzling off the astrolabe's bright blue core like sparks from a fire.

To put it simply, Adwa was a giant workstation. And someone had left it running.

"What is it doing?" I asked.

The WALYA answered, "According to sensor scans, it is

currently executing a query posited to it approximately ten years, four months, and thirteen days ago." It paused, then added, "Someone asked it to do something, and it hasn't yet finished, even though the system's timer for entering hibernation triggered several years back."

"Mesfina," the Ibis said. She squinted at a holodisplay that had winked to life above her head. "The real one. He must've given Adwa an impossible problem, in order to keep it running. If it hibernated, the distress call might have died out."

The oval antigrav lift finally landed in front of us. I nodded, then climbed on board. Besa followed, then the Ibis. I used the Radial to activate the controls. A holointerface appeared on the far side of the lift, with only one available option.

To Operation Command position?

I shrugged. "Why not?" I said, and swiped yes.

The first time you looked at the stars—and I mean really looked at them—what did you see? The space between them? Moons? Satellites or planets or a rocket burning a trail through the sky on its way to some far-off destination? What did you feel? Wonder? Amazement? Overwhelmed? Maybe a little fear? All of the above?

That's what it felt like staring into Adwa's astrolabe. We rose high into the air, dozens and dozens of meters high, until we reached the center of the display. I'd seen smaller versions of astrolabes plenty of times before—Harar Station was full of physical replicas of old navigation equipment that ancient humans used to travel on Old Earth. We even got to see one in action during a school holotrip back on Addis Prime, before I'd ever heard of Old Earth. But those were tiny! Absolute miniatures compared to what hovered in the immense space in front of us.

A flat golden disc the size of a kebele bus spun gently in the air inside of the enormous display cube. Bright dots speckled the space above and below the disc, and hundreds of thin silver rings designed with intricate patterns orbited around it, like rings around a planet. As the lift slowed to a halt a few meters away, I had to crane my neck backward to see the top of the astrolabe. I didn't dare look over the edge of the lift to the bottom. I was afraid to see how high we'd come.

Basically, the astrolabe was huge; we were tiny.

Also, it spoke.

"Welcome! I am Yasisu," a voice spoke. It sounded like Old Earth itself was speaking. The voice was deep and melodical, neither male nor female, but soothing. "New devices detected: wrist communication units and unknown interface."

Why did every AI call the Radial that?

"New astrogation data detected," Yasisu continued. "Possible star lane detected. New locations discovered. Would you like to update the star chart?"

I nodded. Then, when nothing happened, cleared my throat. "Um . . . hi. Yes? Yes, we would? I guess?"

The Ibis shuffled next to me, while Besa sat on her haunches on the other side. Her head was cocked and ears forward, like she'd just heard something curious. My Radial was still engaged, and for once, the WALYA didn't have something snarky to say over the comms. It seemed it was just as awestruck as we were.

The edges of the giant cube—star chart, I guess—pulsed on either side of us. We all gasped as the rings spinning around the astrolabe briefly sped up, then slowed. One ring began to glow, and it expanded in size until it could fit neatly around the golden disc. The bright dots began to grow larger. The Ibis suddenly grabbed my wrist and pointed.

"That's us! That's the Sol System."

And it was, I realized. The dots were stars—we were looking at the galaxy! As we watched, we zoomed into the Sol System and passed by familiar locations. There were the outer planets, the asteroid belt, the inner planets. There was the moon, Luna. There was Sol. There was Debris Town, and—tucked behind it as if it was hiding—there was Old Earth.

"Updating astrogation calculations," Yasisu said. "New location Addis Prime added to database. Five sub-light routes departing Old Earth and arriving at Addis Prime calculated. Seven possible refueling nebulae added to database. Two possible star lanes added to database for tracking and monitoring, one possibly terminating in an unknown star system, the other terminating near Addis Prime. Twenty-two asteroids and planetary moons with above-average mineral deposits added to database. New comm buoys with updated astrogation data are now able to be constructed on the fabrication deck. Update finished. Please note, full station functionality cannot be achieved while grounded. Launch controls are ready."

The star chart zoomed out until I couldn't see the Sol System anymore, but a bright green label and arrow still pointed out Old Earth. Then, in the top-right corner of the cube, toward the front, another dot began to glow. A star. A green label appeared above it, too, and my eyes widened as *Addis Prime* materialized on the label. Five silver lines began to zigzag their way through the cube, connecting the two destinations. One slightly thicker blue line began to do the same, although it was much straighter and more direct.

"Teff of the saints," the Ibis whispered. "No wonder everyone is searching for this place. Did you just see that?"

I exhaled and nodded. "Yeah, that was pretty cool."

"Cool? *Cool?* That was unbelievable!" The Ibis grabbed me by the arm and dragged me toward the guardrail at the edge of the lift, pointing at the star chart. "Do you know how many astrogators would love to have a tenth of the information that thing just dropped on us? Ship routes? Mining? A star lane!" She shook me so intensely that my brain turned to slush. "A star lane!"

"Right, I got it! A star lane." I thought about it for a second. "Hypothetically speaking, if Besa here didn't quite understand what a star lane was, how would you explain it to her? She struggles with new terms and—OUCH!"

I hopped up and down and rubbed my thigh, where one of Besa's spikes had mysteriously jabbed me. The Ibis let out an exasperated sigh and pointed at the thick blue line inside of Yasisu.

"See that? *That* is a star lane. They're like shortcuts through space that ships can take to make journeys quicker, *without* needing special engines like the Menelik drives. Anybody with a standard FTL system can travel them!"

"Anybody," I said slowly, realization dawning, "like a colony ship full of people looking for a new home inside a floating city of junk?"

"Exactly," she said with a smile. "The only problem is, star lanes are always moving because nothing in space remains still. You have to have a way to constantly keep tabs on them."

"Like a giant super-astrolabe computer—" I began.

"And comm buoys scattered throughout space with the updated information," the Ibis finished.

I stared at Yasisu in amazement. This was . . . this was huge. Anybody with a working ship could travel a star lane, and anyone who didn't have a ship could find someone who did and grab a ride. Whatever the cost of a ticket, it would be a hundred times cheaper than what the IU made people pay. You wouldn't have to be superrich in order to board an exclusive luxury vessel? You wouldn't have to be a prince to travel the stars?

"Okay, yeah, this is big. Really big." I thought about it, then engaged the lift to send us back to the ground floor. As it descended, I paced around in circles, trying to figure out what to do next. "We need to find Uncle Moti so he can—"

"So he can what?"

A familiar synthetic voice interrupted me. As the lift reached the ground floor, there was a group of people waiting for us. A man stood in front, wearing a black flight suit and a familiar black-and-silver mask. Mesfina—or the impostor. More soldiers surrounded him, in similar masks though not as fancy. But I only had eyes for the crumpled form lying on the ground several meters in front of the others.

It was Uncle Moti.

"Thank you, Yared," the fake Mesfina said, "but now I'm afraid we'll take it from here."

The Ibis struggled against her arm restraints as Mesfina's soldiers secured her to a giant hunk of unrefined plastere, the stuff spaceships and space stations used to make interior walls.

"Let go of me!" she shouted. "Where are you taking us?"

I sat silent.

We were all on a catwalk that overlooked the Fabrication Deck of Adwa, two decks down from the Astrolabe Deck, where we'd been caught. This was where comm buoys could be manufactured, along with other components needed to maintain the space station while in orbit. Two-thirds of the area was just used for raw material storage, like diranium ore and plastere blocks. They were stacked in storage units that formed aisles on the floor. Loading bots waited nearby in a low-power state, until they were needed to retrieve something.

Conveyor belts lined with robotic arms filled the rest of the area. They floated above us, were installed next to the storage units below us, and were mounted next to us. Raw material was scattered along many of them. Perhaps Adwa had been in the middle of producing something when it crashed. There was surprisingly little damage, however. The station must have kept repairing itself after impact.

At the far end of the deck was a giant fab-bot. They were used to build the large, often dangerous portions of spaceships and stations, like the containment shields for the Menelik drives or exhaust pipes that could turn you into ash within seconds. It squatted at a point where all the conveyor belts converged. It looked like an enormous space spider, with multiple construction limbs extending from the top of it to hover over different belts. The grandfather of all scrappers.

I shuddered but remained silent.

Besa clawed at the rusted green cargo container they'd stuffed her in. Built to transport livestock, there were a few slits cut into the sides to allow them to breathe. I could see Besa pacing around inside, yowling and hurling herself at the walls. The soldiers had gotten her inside by threatening the Ibis and me, but she wasn't happy about it. And she was going to let everyone know about it.

A grav-lift picked up the container and carried it to one of the conveyor belts, where it was dropped none too gently.

I still remained silent.

"Yared!" the Ibis shouted. "Please! What are you doing? Don't just sit there, do something!"

I stared at the dull black catwalk beneath my boots. I knew the Ibis was right—I shouldn't just give up—and yet I couldn't fight. What was I supposed to do when Uncle Moti lay in front of me, silent and still? The only thought rattling around in the chaos of my mind was *Please be okay. Please. Please be okay.*

Another set of boots stepped in front of mine. They nudged Uncle Moti's limp legs out of the way and tapped the catwalk impatiently.

"Come, now," Mesfina said, his voice low and cruel. "You know it doesn't have to be like this. Give me what I want. Hand over the Radial. Don't be like your uncle; you're smarter than that. He refused to cooperate, and look what happened to him!"

I didn't answer. *Please be okay*, I thought.

"Prince Yared—the First! Can't forget to add that little moniker. Prince Yared the First. Axum's beloved son. Well, Lij Yared, my prince, now's the chance for you to earn the praise that has been heaped onto your shoulders."

Please be okay.

A gloved thumb and forefinger grabbed my chin and forced my head up. Mesfina's eyes glared at me from behind his mask. Why? What had I ever done to him?

"Give. Me. The Radial."

The hand fell away, and I looked back down at the floor. Mesfina laughed.

"Look at him. Where's your pride, Yared? Fine. But remember—this is on you."

His words registered faintly in the back of my mind. All I could do was sit there, arms restrained behind my back by one of his soldiers, and stare numbly at Uncle Moti's limp body. He was starting to stir, though he still didn't make a sound. Maybe he'd be okay?

A soldier dragged me to my feet. Mesfina pointed first at the Ibis, then at Besa. "Take a good look, Lij Yared. Memorize their faces. Let them do the same to yours."

He yanked me forward out of his soldier's grip, growling in my face, every word clear despite his mask.

"I want you to watch their last moments. Watch them closely. I want you to see the EXACT second they realize you won't be coming back for them until it's too late. Axum! Saviors of the universe! Come, then—save them. Save them!"

Something glimmered in the corner of my eye. A trinket on a chain. I only saw it for an instant, but that was enough. I'd seen it before.

"You know what's weird?" I said quietly. "Forget about

me—I can understand why you'd take it out on me. You've been working for years to earn a tenth of the recognition and privilege I just stumbled into. I get it. But the Ibis? Besa? Are they guilty, too? What about everybody in Debris Town, all those families terrorized by your pretend pirate ships? All the kids that went hungry because the IU, parasites though they may be, won't send any relief? All because everybody was terrified of the big bad pirates in Debris Town. What about them?"

I took a step forward, ignoring the soldiers leveling their weapons at me. "No, you don't care about them. You don't care about anybody but yourself. At the end of the day, you and I are the same. Just two boys with a little power and no idea what to do with it. Isn't that right, Jemal?"

The Ibis gasped so loud I heard it from across the room. Some of the soldiers milled around, confused as Mesfina— or, to be accurate, Mesfina's *son*—laughed and pulled off the ornate black-and-silver mask to reveal Jemal's face twisted in bitter amusement.

"How long have you known?"

I shrugged. "I suspected it after seeing the video. He was your father, wasn't he? But I couldn't be sure until just now. You two have the same eyes. And I wondered why you'd need a voice synth in your mask. No one from Axum would question someone who made a vow to recover part of our home, right? After all, Uncle Moti and Aunt Yas made vows. If the hero of Adwa wanted to keep his face covered until he returned home, that was honorable, right?"

I shook my head. "And then there was the necklace. You're wearing the same one."

"That was the only thing they could find," Jemal said, speaking softly. "And that was pure luck. It was scorched and tangled on a piece of debris some scrappers found."

I sighed. "Jemal, I'm sorry—"

He scoffed. "No, you aren't. Not yet. But you will be."

I was yanked around again by the soldier restraining me. He marched me to the edge of the catwalk so that I could see both the Ibis and Besa now on opposite ends of the Fabrication Deck. Both on conveyor belts. Both were watching me, frightened, angry, and helpless. In the corner of my eye, I could see Uncle Moti's prone form.

You can be a rocket or you can be a shield.

And that's when I knew what I had to do.

"We have a responsibility," I whispered.

Jemal stepped up next to me, and I turned and glared at him. "Fine," I said. "You can have the Radial. Just . . . don't hurt my friends."

He nodded at the soldier behind me, who released my arms. Jemal then held out his hand expectantly. I hesitated, then extended my wrists and whispered, "Disengage."

With a barely audible click, both bracelets unsnapped and fell, and Jemal snatched them up greedily. He fit them over his own wrists, sighing with pleasure when they snapped closed and a bright golden light began to emanate from them. The other soldiers took a step forward, mesmerized by the unfolding spirals, just like I was when I first put on the Radial.

"Magnificent," he murmured. "Adwa, activate!"

The entire room began to shake as the astrolabe space station—for the first time in over a decade—began to power up fully. The floors vibrated, the walls trembled, and everything not fastened down (including one handsome prince and his friends) was at risk of smashing into both.

When would I have a better chance to escape, I hear you asking. What a great question.

I hopped over the edge of the catwalk and dropped to the conveyor belt beneath, and was halfway to Besa by the time anyone noticed or shouted after me. I slid to a stop around the corner of the cargo container just as the soldiers began to fire.

"Yared!" Jemal shouted, fury in his voice.

"One moment!" I called back. "Be right with you! Just . . . sabotaging your plans. Hold, please!"

Besa whined as she pawed at the hinges from the inside. "Hold on, girl. I got you," I said, frantically pulling at the mag-locks. Finally, I managed to pull one lock free, sliding it off to clatter onto the floor. A yowl was the only warning I got as Besa slammed into the door. I dove away as the whole thing flew off, taking out a pair of soldiers who were running down the belt toward us.

"I know, I know," I said, climbing onto her back. "You hate tight spaces."

"Mrowr."

"Yes, you don't deserve that."

"Mrowr."

"After we rescue the Ibis, launch Adwa, defeat Jemal and his band of spawn campers—"

"Mrowr."

"Yeah, I hate spawn campers. But once we do all that, then yes, I will take you to get your spikes polished. Spa day. But first . . ."

Besa leapt into the air, bounding from conveyor belt to conveyor belt as she made her way across the room. She skidded to a stop just in front of the fab-bot. I didn't have my Radial to communicate with it directly, but who needed to do things the easy way?

The master switch was nearly the size of a small child. I threw myself against it, while Besa leapt and pounced on the soldiers trying to pin us down. With a roar, she twisted and brandished her spikes. Together we scrambled toward the chunk of plastere the Ibis was chained to.

Besa, with a swipe of her claws, shredded the restraints.

Jemal stomped toward us on a conveyor belt directly overhead, his mask in one hand and the other pointing at me. "Get him!" he screamed. "He's making a fool out of all of you! And someone bring me my exo!"

That wasn't good. I was going to need some help.

"Grab Uncle Moti and then get to the *Menen*," I said, sliding off of Besa. I boosted the Ibis onto the lioness's back. "And tell WALYA I'm going to need backup but to wait for my signal."

She nodded. "What are you going to do?"

I sprinted to the service lift and slammed the button for the Astrolabe Deck. I grinned just before the hatchway spiraled shut.

"I'm going to lead them to the arena. There, I can go be a shield."

CHAPTER FIFTEEN

So, here it is. Yared Heywat's final rule for the intergalactic hologuide to winning your battle royale match. You ready for it? Listen close, it's a two-parter: The best players know when to run and hide, and—

SMASH.

"You hear that, Yared?" Jemal's voice boomed through his exo's external speakers. "That's your destiny arriving. Say hello to the Hyena-2. Managed to get my hands on one, and let me tell you, this thing will crush ships. You can't hide forever, and it'll only be worse for you when I do get my hands on you."

The massive claws of the Hyena-2 swiped through an assembly tower, showering the area with debris. I ducked, even though Jemal stomped and attacked indiscriminately. Scrappers and locust drones alike went flying as he rampaged through the arena.

SMASH.

Wow. So rude. This is why the galaxy is the way it is today—nobody wants to let people finish their train of thought in the middle of a dramatic fight scene. Not that there was much fighting going on. I was taking part one of my own advice seriously—by hiding!

What? Don't make that face. I know you don't believe me, but you have to trust me on this—you can't run, glide, or jump into every fight that comes looking for you. At least not right away. Take your time. Scope out the arena. There will be players and bosses and weird, plantlike zombies and murderous exos piloted by an older kid who you thought could be your friend.

So run. Hide. Figure out a strategy to take your opponents down. And when you're ready, take it to them.

SMASH.

Simple, right?

That's what I was trying to do at the moment, as I hid behind an assembly hive in the far corner of the Gibe Arena. I was out of breath, my lungs almost ready to call it quits.

Adwa slowly rose into Old Earth's atmosphere, the light from the sun piercing the shield keeping us safe, throwing the arena into constantly shifting shadows. Most of it fell on the stage, and I stared longingly at the hatchway that led back to Yasisu.

SMASH.

I could hear Jemal in his Hyena-2 stomping around nearby, but I couldn't see him. Not that he was trying to be stealthy. I felt bad for the scrapper bots. Somehow—and don't make me think too deeply about it—I'd come to grow fond of the bug-like robots. They just wanted to make a home and raise their little creepy bug-bot children like the rest of the galaxy. Maybe it was all of my time hanging out with Besa and arguing with the WAL—

SMASH.

The assembly hive I was hiding behind disintegrated in a shower of scrapper parts. The vicious, leering face of the Hyena-2 loomed over me, enormous jaws crunching on scrappers, locust drones, and assembly hives all at once. The exo bent until I could see the furious gleam in Jemal's eye through his helmet.

"Found you," he said, and his arm shot forward.

I shouted in pain as, for the second time in as many days, I found myself dangling helplessly upside down. (Had it really only been two days? Time flies when you're searching for a missing space station module.)

"You know what your problem is?" Jemal's voice crackled as he lumbered through the demolished ruins of the scrapper hives, carrying me like a sack of teff. "Your problem, Yared, is you don't have any ambition. No drive. You could've been great! It's a whole galaxy out there that we've been blocked from. How many worlds have we missed out on exploring? How many stars have been extinguished while we work like dogs for people that toss us scraps and expect us to be grateful?"

"You said your mother was the leader of one of Old Earth's biggest factions!" I shouted. "Isn't she one of the ones tossing scraps?"

We stopped in the crater where I fought the locust drones. Jemal lifted me so the Hyena-2 faceshield filled my view. "My mother," he snarled, "was a leader of a group of WORKERS! She led a FACTION OF WORKERS! She fought for better pay and a higher standard of living for the people she worked with, people who toiled in the dark and cold of space to build yachts and luxury accommodations on space stations. And you know what the IU called her? A rabble-rouser. A problem. Kicked her and the other workers off the job just because they wanted to be safe. Replaced them and pushed the construction job through."

Jemal took a deep breath, the strain on his face visible as he closed his eyes. "The space station that my mother worked on . . . the one my *father* commanded . . . crashed."

It took me several seconds to make the connection. Then my face fell.

"Adwa," I whispered. "Your mother built Adwa . . . and your father—"

"Died. Serving the people who left him behind. The people who left the IU in charge."

As frightening and disturbing as his actions had been, I could almost . . . almost . . . understand why Jemal did it. Almost. "Is this what your mother wants? Do you think you're any different from the people you hate?" I asked, squeezing my words through gritted teeth.

Jemal's face tightened. "It doesn't matter what she would have wanted. She died not long after my father did."

"And you think your father would be proud?"

All of a sudden, I was being hurled through the air. Everything spun in a blur, until I crashed to the floor and skidded several meters. The broken remains of a scrapper hive stopped my slide. I grunted in pain as the air whooshed out of my lungs.

"My father," Jemal growled, "made his choice. He gave his life to Axum, to *duty*, and what did that get him? Hmm? What did that get him? Nothing! He doesn't even have a grave!"

He was shouting now, the Hyena-2 jerking around in spasms as the older boy grew angrier. "He chose his mission over us. His family. Do you know how that feels? To be second favorite to an empire that abandoned him?"

I glanced at the stage, and the hatch that led to the

Astrolabe Deck. It was so far away. I scooted back, putting the broken hive between me and the exo. It offered very little protection, but anything was better than nothing. There was no telling when Jemal's fury would erupt again. I needed whatever head start I could get.

"The Werari—" I started to say, but Jemal sent the exo hurtling forward. He backhanded the broken hive so viciously that I had to tumble sideways or be flattened.

"The Werari," he sneered. "Always the Werari. Great job, Dad! You kept a navigational supercomputer out of the hands of a pack of slobbering colonizers, but guess what else happened? The rest of the solar system suffered, too! Your precious *Hope*, the overcrowded slums on Old Earth. No one could escape with Adwa gone, and that meant the IU could move in and red-tape everyone to death. Well, I'm sick of it. Whoever controls Adwa controls the galaxy, and I plan on being that person. As soon as we dock with Axum, the stars are mine."

A streak of light hurtled over the arena's shields. We were breaking through the clouds and shooting into the upper atmosphere of Old Earth.

I smiled.

"How?" I asked.

Jemal paused in the middle of whatever tirade he was about to launch into. "What?"

"How are you going to dock with Axum if you can't interface with Yasisu?"

He looked dumbfounded, then flipped over the arms of the exo. The Radial bracelets were gone. "What . . . ? How . . . ? Where did they go?" He turned on me, but I shrugged and pointed off to the left, where a group of scrapper bots were fleeing toward the arena wall.

"I'm gonna give you a primer on one of the biggest rules in the Yared hologuide—never get flanked. Don't disturb scrapper hives, remember? They love building technology into their nests."

Jemal bellowed in frustration, and the Hyena-2 lumbered off. I waited until he was gone, then slipped the Radial I'd palmed onto my wrist and flicked it open. Did I feel bad blaming the scrappers for my deception? Yes. Did I cackle a bit watching Jemal try to catch the elusive little things? Absolutely.

"And tip number three," I whispered to myself. "Subterfuge is a champion's best friend."

A roar of anger followed soon after. I let out a little yelp as the Hyena-2 thundered back across the arena toward me. Not enough subterfuge! I turned and sprinted toward the stage. I could hear Jemal getting nearer with every passing second.

The stage was so close . . . just a few . . . more . . . meters . . .

The Hyena-2 landed in front of me with a thud. Jemal laughed as the exo crouched down on the stage. "Come on, Yared. You think I couldn't figure out your little plan? Better luck next time."

I mumbled something into the cloud of dust that was still settling from his landing.

"What?" he said, frowning.

I looked up and smiled. "I said, you never let me finish the final rule of Yared's Intergalactic Hologuide. The best players know when to run and hide, and attack when the odds are in their favor."

Jemal scoffed. "Sorry, my *prince*. You're on the losing side this time."

"Tell that to my friend," I said, nodding at the shields above our head.

A streak of light brighter than any star flew like a missile right at us. I flicked open the Radial and spread my arms wide. "WALYA," I said, "Sengis Punch!"

The arena shields shattered in a shower of sparks. Alarms wailed and lights flashed. Before Jemal could move, the WALYA's fist slammed into the larger exo. The Hyena-2 rocketed backward at the force of the impact, rolling over the edge and falling off the stage. I grinned. Guess he didn't figure out my plan after all.

"Greetings, squishy one," the WALYA said. "It appears you are in need of assistance."

"Right on schedule," I said, leaping onto the stage and climbing inside the exo. I walked to the edge and stared down at the Hyena-2. The left side was completely caved in. Jemal lay still. The readouts flashing across the WALYA's HUD said he was fine, just stunned. Good. Didn't want him getting in the way for this next part.

"You know what your problem is, Jemal?" I asked. "Instead of being responsible for your own actions, you think the galaxy owes you. Somebody once told me that those with privilege should wield it like a warrior would a weapon because you might end up hurting someone without realizing. And that someone might be yourself."

"Powerful monologue, human," the WALYA said, "but impending doom has not slowed to accommodate your speech. So . . . if you would . . ."

I was two seconds away from selling the exo for scrap metal.

The suit powered up all my protective systems, and just in the nick of time. Alerts started flooding the HUD—low oxygen, gravity failure, environmental hazards. Not to mention what I could see approaching through the shattered remnants of the shields.

"Scans are showing impact with numerous foreign objects is imminent," the exo said.

"Debris Town," I said grimly.

The refugee space colony lay directly in the path of Adwa's route to Harar Station. I only hoped the Ibis had gotten there fast enough. If the residents were all aboard the *Hope*, maybe no one would get hurt. I opened a comm channel and prayed to the stars we were in range.

Comm signal interference flashed on the HUD.

I groaned. "WALYA, we have to get beyond Debris Town and warn the *Hope*. Is there an escape pod aboard that we can use?"

The AI was silent for a split second. "All escape pods appear to be missing, perhaps due to the crash."

Of course. I'd completely forgotten. So how were we going to—

"But there is one other option, though it is risky and entirely humanlike in its execution."

More alerts popped up on my HUD as Debris Town grew closer. I shook my head. "Fine, what is it?"

"Due to the additional profiles accumulated recently—Sengis, Augur Hawk, and Golden Wolf—it is theoretically possible to accelerate past Adwa Station using all three, charting a path through the refugee city ahead of us."

I had to stop and think about what WALYA actually said. Even then I still couldn't believe it. That . . . wasn't possible. Right?

"You want me," I said slowly, "to jump into space and . . . parkour through Debris Town?"

"A suboptimal comparison, but for the sake of your vocabulary . . . yes."

Ten more red alerts popped up. Time was running out, so what choice did I have?

"You can be a rocket," I said to myself, "or you can be a shield. Okay. Let's do it."

"Are you sure this is going to work?" I asked.

The WALYA paused for a tenth of a second, then said, "Apologies, but all data suggests it is well past the time to be asking that."

"Fair enough," I said.

We were standing on the hull plating of the exterior of Adwa, just a few paces from the broken shields over the Gibe Arena. The plating was pitted and scarred, though whether that was from crashing into Old Earth or from launching back into space after a decade of inaction, I couldn't tell you. What I could tell you was that it was absolutely terrifying standing and watching the leading edges of Debris Town rushing toward us. The only thing that kept me out there, and not ducking back inside to hide with the scrapper bots, was the hulking edges of the *Hope* peeking out from behind the other satellites, broken ships, and space junk. If I couldn't get through all of that . . . well, I didn't want to think about it.

"Systems launching in T-minus ten seconds," the WALYA announced.

I took a deep breath, then nodded. Teff of the saints, we were really doing this. Faces flashed through my mind—Uncle Moti, the Ibis, my parents, Aunt Yas. The families aboard the *Hope.* Even Balamba Ras and . . . wow, I couldn't believe I was saying this, but even Jemal.

Was I angry at the hurt, all the pain, all the chaos his deception had caused?

Yes.

". . . six . . . five . . . four . . ."

Did I want the boy—who was hurting inside—to die?

No. Never that.

". . . three . . . two . . . one . . ."

And with that last thought shining in my mind, I dropped into a crouch—

". . . go!"

—and shouted, "Sengis Punch!"

I exploded off of the hull, shooting through the black of space like a comet. Our first target was a malfunctioning comm buoy at the forefront of Debris Town. Instead of punching it, I would have to use my hands to slightly adjust my trajectory. A tightly packed group of old broadcast satellites followed that. I would have to time it just right in order to squeeze through. There was the comm buoy. I grabbed it and used the momentum to redirect myself toward the satellites, and let go . . .

"Augur Hawk: One Thousand Wings!" As I spoke, the WALYA switched profiles. The energy wings with their gravity webbing appeared on my shoulders, the feathers glowing electric blue. With one powerful flap, I was speeding off in a new direction, the wings folded behind me, blazing like a cone of fire. I entered a spin, just narrowly slipping through the satellites. A piece of metal glanced off my side, but I managed to avoid disaster and squeezed through the slim passage.

"Booster rocket fragments incoming," the WALYA warned.

I nodded. "Golden Wolf: Pursuit!"

The wings disappeared, replaced by maneuvering thrusters on my arms and legs. An Old Earth booster rocket floated in several pieces directly in my path. Any ordinary exo would've been smashed to pieces if they collided with the huge curved metal shards, but the Golden Wolf was built for quick agility, just like the Augur Hawk was built for speed. I sprang off of each, using the maneuvering thrusters to quickly redirect myself up one, flip over another, and spring off a third.

"Alert," the WALYA said. "A malfunctioning solar collector has drifted into target coordinates. Avoidance will result in high casualties."

"What does that mean?" I shouted.

"To clarify, if Adwa collides with the solar collector, irreparable damage will be caused to both the space station and the *Hope*, which lies in the way of collision debris. However, attempting to interfere decreases the likelihood of survival."

"For the station?"

"For you."

I gulped as I sprang off of the last booster rocket and saw it. The solar collector was a floating rhombus connected to an enormous solar sail, a mirrorlike cloth nearly as big as Adwa. And there beyond it was the *Hope*.

The exterior of the colony ship was a maze of activity. Tiny ships swarmed over the hull. Cargo transports loaded supplies, maintenance cruisers performed last-minute repairs, and I even saw a fuel tanker approaching. The giant crane, luckily, had been removed, but it still floated too close for comfort. This had all the indications of a disaster in the making.

"Recommend abandoning approach," the WALYA said. "There is a chance the *Hope* will see the solar collector and relocate on its own, thus rendering our efforts irrelevant. By doing so, they will also avoid collision with Adwa."

I almost deactivated my thrusters, but I hesitated. "What kind of a chance?"

"Well . . ." said the WALYA.

I raised my eyebrows. Was it reluctant?

"Less than five percent."

My heart sank. That wasn't a chance. That was a hope. A prayer. If I sat back and did nothing, was I any better than Jemal? The answer to that made me uncomfortable.

I couldn't let that happen. I *wouldn't* let that happen. "No. Stick with the plan."

The WALYA sighed. (Can AIs sigh? Or is it like . . . some thermal exhaust that happened after they'd eaten too many—you know what? Never mind. I don't want to know.)

"Accumulated historical data suggested you would say that. Very well, the alternative is to destroy the solar collector at . . . *this* marked location. Doing so will slightly alter its debris trajectory and possibly even alert the *Hope*. But you will not—"

"Copy that," I interrupted. Some things you have to face without knowing the odds.

I took a deep breath, counted to three, then slammed the controls forward. I had one shot at this. One opportunity to be a shield for people who were used to those with privilege abandoning their responsibilities when the going got tough. Like the IU. Like I used to do. Well . . . no more.

"Augur Hawk!"

I needed to pick up speed.

"Golden Wolf!"

I was slightly off trajectory. Readjust. And, when the moment was right . . .

"Sengis—

It was time to strike.

"—Punch!"

The solar collector disintegrated into metal shards and ripped cloth as the WALYA slammed into it. The remnants of the old technology shot off in all directions, save for two—nothing flew toward the *Hope*, and nothing flew toward Adwa.

I'd done it. Wait. We'd done it. WE'D DONE IT! And even better . . .

". . . to WALYA-1, *Menen* to WALYA-1, do you copy? Over."

"Hey!" I said, relieved beyond measure. "I can hear you!"

"Yared?" It was the Ibis. "Was that . . . ? Of course that was you."

I grinned, then sobered up. The whole reason we'd come this far was to pass along a message. There was an alert flashing on my HUD, but I ignored it. "Hey, you've got to tell Aunt Yas—Adwa Station has launched and is coming this way. They need to move, and fast!"

A different voice cut in. "Yared, what do you mean coming this way?" Uncle Moti asked.

I suppressed the urge to ask him questions—How was he doing? Was he hurt? Had he reunited with Aunt Yas?—and instead told them about the battle with Jemal. They listened in stunned silence as I ran down the launch, and the hair-raising attempt to break through the communication jam. More alerts were piling up on my HUD, but I dismissed them all. I'd have plenty of time to read them in a second.

"You took a giant risk, my boy," Uncle Moti said. "But I know why you did it."

"Now just come on back to the *Hope* and we'll get out of the way," the Ibis added.

I swallowed, a fluttering feeling settling in my stomach as the adrenaline rush from smashing the solar collector faded away. This was the part the WALYA had tried to warn me about. The odds I hadn't wanted to face. "See, the thing is . . . I can't."

Silence. Then:

"What do you mean you can't?" Uncle Moti exploded.

"Well . . ."

"Yared Heywat, you'd better—"

"The momentum from destroying the solar collector sent me too far out. I'm . . . drifting."

More silence. And then the Ibis spoke. "That's not funny," she said. "Hurry up and—"

"I can't. I don't have the power." Alerts were flashing left and right on my HUD. The panic I'd been trying to fend off was starting to settle in. I could barely breathe, and suddenly, the helmet felt so hot. So heavy. There was a number, big and bright and red on my HUD, and somewhere far away I could hear the WALYA trying to get my attention. But the only thing I could focus on was how that number kept growing and growing. It was important for some reason.

Distance from target.

That's right. I was drifting farther and farther away from everyone. From the *Menen*. From the *Hope*. From home.

Something fell down my face. Tears? Weird. I couldn't be sad right now . . . I was a hero! Yared the Gr8 had saved the day, thank you very much. I'd been a shield, not a rocket, and no one could take that away from me. So these tears? They were ridiculous. Right?

Right?

So why did they keep falling?

The only sound I could hear was my own panicked breath. And it hit me. I didn't want this to be the end. I didn't want to float forever. I didn't want to be alone. I . . .

THUNK.

Something crashed into me, snaking around my shoulders and squeezing tight.

"I'm tired of you being the hero," came an angry snarl. The Hyena-2—battered and crumpled in spots—leered at me through my helmet. Its massive jaws were clamped on the WALYA. (Terrifying, even at this moment.)

"Jemal?"

The older boy glared at me. "You were going to throw your life away, just like he did."

I didn't have to ask who *he* was. Mesfina's patch—his father's patch, of a golden flat-topped mountain surrounded by stars—glinted on the exo's chest armor. Instead, I shook my head. "Sacrifice isn't throwing your life away. Not when it's for people you care about."

The oversized boosters on the Hyena-2's legs fired, and Jemal muttered something as he used his thrusters to turn me right side up, facing the *Hope.*

"Sounds like something Dad would say," he grumbled, and I grinned.

The colony ship had begun to move, veering out of harm's way. I let out a sigh of relief. Everyone would be safe, and just in the nick of time. Only a few kilometers away, Adwa emerged from Debris Town, on its way back to Axum.

I closed my eyes. "Next family trip," I said, "I get to choose the destination."

CHAPTER SIXTEEN

Silence awaited me as I limped out of the lift onto the Walk of Sheba. Besa followed, refusing to let me out of her sight. Our footprints glittered for an instant before fading. We were early. For once, I appreciated the solitude. Not that I didn't want to hang out with my friends or talk with my family—I did. I never wanted to be separated from them again. But coming up here by myself, even if it was only for an instant, reminded me of just how much my friends and family meant to me. It also made me think about how fortunate I was.

Privilege.

A month had passed since Adwa reconnected with Harar Station. One standard month of testing, analyzing, rebuilding, and hoping. Lots and lots of hoping. Today was the day we were supposed to find out if our hard work paid off.

The giant vidscreen blinked on, revealing the black of space around the Axum capital. Stars winked as ships passed in front of them, some heading in-system, some leaving. Hopefully, after today, the Sol-Luna System would stretch out into the galaxy once more.

The lift hatchway hissed open behind me. "It is puzzling why humans design such inefficient entranceways. Why does it spiral open? My calculations indicate that an energy savings of 0.79 percent would be gained if the hatch simply slid open."

I sighed as the WALYA walked up to stand next to me, the exo folding its arms and brooding. (I guess. Can sentient AIs brood?)

"Because it looks cool."

The exo nodded as if it expected me to say that. "Energy inefficiency is 'cool.' I am learning so much about humanity . . . and I regret it."

"Why are you here again?"

The WALYA slumped. "Your human chefs banned me from the kitchens, and your astrogator companion threatened to make me help her rehome scrapper assembly hives."

"Poor thing," I said, wincing in sympathy. "The Ibis can be—"

The hatch hissed open again.

"The Ibis can be what?" The girl walked in, back in her black Axum flight suit, her wrist comm active as cones of data floated above it. She flicked one away, minimized another, and enlarged a third. By the time she'd reached us, all the cones were stacked on top of one another. She tapped out a quick command before collapsing them down to a single ticker that circled her wrist. The Ibis looked at the WALYA and me, raising one eyebrow.

"You were saying?" she asked.

"I was saying," I began, "that the Ibis can be an excellent role model and mentor for those willing to put in the— OOF!" I staggered backward dramatically as she elbowed me. "Hey, I'm *injured*."

Turns out you can't go through as many high-speed maneuvers in zero gravity as I did without proper training and conditioning. Destroying the solar collector put more strain on my body than I'd ever felt. I think I heard the doctors faint once or twice while looking at my medical chart.

On the plus side, Axum engineers were excited about the potential for more exos that could do the same. They were planning a whole WALYA-class series of power armors, ones that might even be able to stand up to the Meshenitai.

Not that I needed one . . . my WALYA was more than enough for me.

The Ibis shook a fist at me. "You're not injured that seriously . . . yet," she threatened.

I limped behind the WALYA for protection, who was absolutely confused by our interaction. The Ibis and I traded insults for a bit, until the hatch opened again and in walked Uncle Moti. He was a bit out of breath, as if he'd run all the way here.

"Did I miss it?" he asked.

We all shook our heads. ("Negative," said the WALYA.) I watched as he wiped sweat from his face, searching for any lingering effects from his time in captivity. The doctors said he would be fine, but sometimes I'd catch him wincing when he thought no one was looking. I was trying to do better at checking on the people around me. Especially the ones closest to me. You never knew who could be hurting inside.

Uncle Moti caught me looking at him and gave me a thumbs-up. "Why are you so out of breath?" I asked.

"Got a message from Yas," he said with a sheepish grin.

"Oh! How did it go?"

The *Hope* was the very first ship to fly the star lane Adwa had discovered. Aunt Yas and the people of Debris Town traveled to Addis Prime, where they would be given homes and support on the colony. Along the way, the *Hope* dropped comm buoys that would map the entirety of the star lane, and send data back to Adwa so other ships could access the time-saving route.

Uncle Moti sighed. "Everyone's safe and happy, though they're remaining on Addis Prime for a little while longer. They found some asteroids with mineral deposits, and they're taking some samples."

"And Jemal?"

"Doing what he's told. Yas is actually happy to have him along."

It took some time to figure out how to deal with Jemal. The older boy had saved me after all, and apparently if you save a prince that counts for something. On the other hand, it didn't erase all the harm he'd caused and the lives he'd impacted. Uncle Moti and my parents had debated it for weeks and gotten nowhere, before Aunt Yas finally stomped into the briefing room and slammed a weird-looking piece of machinery on table.

"That boy you sent to me for maintenance detail," she had said, "fixed a thirty-year-old hydraulic system that my engineers had written off as dead. This is the same boy who tweaked his own powered exoskeleton and was the only one capable of saving my nephew. You want to know what to do with him? Give him to me for the Addis Prime trip. Let him help others by doing what he always wanted to do—leave the system."

And so Jemal was put into Aunt Yas's care. I was happy for him. Sometimes you had to get away from the place where grief made its home. I couldn't bring myself to hate him for his actions. I think Aunt Yas said it best when I asked her why she'd volunteered to take in someone who'd hurt so many people.

"Do we want to hurt him or heal him?" she'd asked me. "I look at him and, but for a twist of fate, I see you. What if— saints forbid—something had happened to Moti and you were left all alone, with no one watching out for you? Who would you have become? So yes, I will take him in because I would've wanted someone to do the same for you."

I was glad to hear Jemal was doing well. I really was.

I began to turn back to the viewing panels, when I caught something in Uncle Moti's expression. "Was there anything else that Aunt Yas said?"

He cleared his throat and . . . was he blushing? "Boy, that is grown folks' business, and you can just keep looking at the stars."

Everyone began to laugh, when suddenly the Ibis was flailing one arm to get our attention. She stared at her wrist comm. "Shhh, it's here!" She tapped in a command, waited for an answer, then pointed to a particular panel. "There!"

It was hard to see at first. Nearly impossible. But after a few moments and several magnification requests, a blinking light began to grow in the distance. I held my breath. Uncle Moti muttered under his, probably without even realizing it. The Ibis bounced up and down on her toes, while the WALYA and Besa remained perfectly still. When the object finally became large enough to view on-screen, a giant smile crossed my face.

When Adwa came fully online, we sent out a drone to fly the *other* star lane, the one that terminated near an unknown star system. It was a test, really. The Azmari-engineers weren't sure if the drone would survive the flight; they were just planning on collecting data from it for as long as it could transmit.

It did more than just survive.

Two days ago, long-range scanners detected its return. Which . . . shouldn't have been possible, since it was designed for a one-way flight.

Someone had sent it back—with a two-word message in tow.

"Find us."

ABOUT THE AUTHORS

Kwame Mbalia is a husband, father, writer, a *New York Times* bestselling author, and a former pharmaceutical metrologist, in that order. His debut middle-grade novel, *Tristan Strong Punches a Hole in the Sky*, was awarded a Coretta Scott King Author Honor and it—along with the sequels *Tristan Strong Destroys the World* and *Tristan Strong Keeps Punching*—is published by Rick Riordan Presents/Disney-Hyperion. He is the coauthor of *Last Gate of the Emperor* with Prince Joel Makonnen, from Scholastic Press, and the editor of the #1 *New York Times* bestselling anthology *Black Boy Joy*, published by Delacorte Press. A Howard University graduate and a Midwesterner now in North Carolina, he survives on dad jokes and Cheez-Its. Visit him online at kwamembalia.com.

Prince Joel Makonnen is the great-grandson of His Imperial Majesty Emperor Haile Selassie I, the last emperor of Ethiopia. He is an attorney and the cofounder of Old World/ New World, a media and entertainment company focused on telling powerful African stories that inspire global audiences through film, TV, and books. He lives with his wife, Ariana, in Los Angeles. Visit him online at princeyoel.com.